Pasmore

David Storey

Pasmore

E. P. DUTTON & CO., INC.

NEW YORK

PART I

One

He woke to find the room full of sunlight.

A dull pain throbbed between his eyes. His face was covered with sweat.

When he turned on his side he saw that Kay was still asleep, her face sunk down in the pillows, almost hidden.

The children, presumably, had been in to open the curtains. He could hear them crashing about in their room at the front of the house. The alarm hadn't rung yet. It was almost seven o'clock.

When he went down to the kitchen his eldest daughter, Susan, appeared on the stairs. 'Are you making some tea?' she said.

'I hope to,' he said.

Her bare feet pattered down behind him.

'Did you come in and open the curtains?' he said.

'Yes,' she said. 'I heard you call.'

'Call?'

She stood by the stove, watching him light the kettle. Her head was little higher than the ring.

'You must have been asleep,' she said.

'Yes,' he said, and added, 'What was I calling?'

'I don't know,' she said. 'I didn't hear.'

'Well,' he said, 'next time you'd better listen.'

'Yes,' she said and smiled.

He went through from the kitchen, at the back of the house, to the hall and opened the front door.

An old man with a dog was walking in the gardens. He glanced up at the opening of the door, then he turned off along the footpath which led to the wooden shelter at the centre of the square. Here he sat down, his hands clasped on a stick, the dog lying by his feet. A pool of sunlight lit up the hut. The rest of the square, because of the trees, was still in shadow.

It was very quiet.

He picked up the newspaper from the step and went out to the van and tried the doors.

'What is it?' his daughter said. She had come to the doorway.

'I've left the window open,' he said. 'All night.'

He looked inside. The back was full of children's seats, toys, domestic appliances, and various parts of the van itself, a headlamp, tyres, a carburettor which, replaced, had never been thrown away. His name had been written in the dust along one side. 'Please clean this van.' 'Pass Along Please.' 'Pass More.'

'Is it all right?' she said.

'Yes,' he said.

He opened the door, raised the window, then locked it.

When he went in she had made the tea.

He took it up to Kay.

She was sitting up in bed, her cheeks flushed, her eyes still drowsy. The other two children sat on the bed.

'You're already up,' she said when he came in. 'I didn't hear you.'

'Oh,' he said. 'They've been making the usual racket.'

'Well,' she said to the children, 'clear off. We haven't got up yet.'

'Are you getting up soon?' they said.

'Yes,' she said. 'Hop it.'

Then, a few moments later, they heard them in the kitchen.

'We left the van unlocked,' he said.

'Is it all right?'

She glanced up; her eyes, dazed, were scarcely open.

'Yes,' he said.

'Are you all right?' she said.

'Yes.'

He sat on the bed, unmoving.

'Is anything the matter?' she said.

'No,' he said, and shook his head.

He got up without adding anything further and went down to the children.

Normally he took them to school, on his way to college. The eldest child, Susan, went to a primary school a few streets away, the younger girl, Cynthia, to a nursery round the corner. Kenneth, the boy, who was scarcely two, stayed at home with Kay.

Now, however, when they were ready she had said, 'I'll take them. In the van. It won't be any trouble.'

'I'll be all right,' he said.

'Are you sure?' she asked him.

He turned away, pulling on his coat.

She came to the door to see them off. The old man was still sitting in the hut, the dog by his feet. The sunlight now had faded.

At the corner of the square he waved.

The two girls walked behind him, holding hands.

When he'd left them at their schools he set off down the hill towards Bloomsbury and the college. The traffic now was thick, moving into town. The sky had clouded. He ran once to board a bus, found it was full, and continued walking.

The college had formerly been a working-men's institute for further education. It was a mixture of old brick buildings and new concrete tenements, faced, in one instance, with Portland stone. The history school occupied a corner of the oldest building of all, and could only be reached by crossing two yards and climbing several flights of stairs.

Coles was waiting for him when he arrived, standing across the corridor from the room they shared, staring down into the yard outside – already, by this time, full of parked cars. He looked up when he heard his steps, gazing one way then another, the light glinting from his glasses.

'I wouldn't go in there,' he said, indicating the door. ''Crombie's unpacking his belongings.'

'What belongings?' he said.

'Oh.' His friend's stooped and rather ravaged figure trembled and, clutching his briefcase more closely to him, he added, 'The usual sort of thing.' He smiled eerily, his eyes distorted behind the heavy lenses, to indicate that he himself felt in no way put out.

'What are we supposed to do?' he said. 'Hang about out here?'

'Well,' Coles said, 'I shouldn't think so,' his smile widening, his eyes dilating, almost disappearing.

He followed Pasmore in, relieved.

Bending over the desk in the centre of the room was Abercrombie. A small, dapper man with a neat, goatee beard, he was unpacking a rucksack. A pair of boots, several lengths of rope, a wind-cheater and various cans and packets were laid out on the desk top. Also scattered there were his squash racquet and his shorts and plimsolls.

'Had a marvellous weekend, man,' he said, scarcely glancing up. He had, very slightly, a Scottish accent.

6

'Where's that?' Coles said.

'Oh, Wales, man.' He indicated the boots: they were studded, perhaps excessively, for climbing. 'Nearly broke my bloody neck.'

'Pity,' he said.

'What?' He glanced across.

Pasmore indicated the desk. The room, normally, was used for tutorials and marking. It looked down into the yard of the college and, beyond that, to the street outside.

Abercrombie had smiled. 'Oh, I'll soon clear this off, old man,' he said.

'I'll do it for you,' Pasmore said.

He was surprised himself at his own intentness.

The next moment he had seized the boots, the rope, the wind-cheater, the rucksack and most of the cans, the racquet, the shorts and the plimsolls, and, opening the door with his foot, stepped past the startled Coles and flung them down the corridor outside.

'Why should we be continually subjected to these manifestations of your childish bloody mind?' he said.

Abercrombie regarded him for a moment in silence. It was difficult to imagine how the incident had begun.

'I don't know, man,' he said. 'Perhaps these manifestations of my childish bloody mind might do you a bit of good. It seems to me you've been shut up in this place for far too long.' He indicated the college.

'I've been shut up, all right,' he said. 'Shut up with nuts like you, Abercrombie.'

'Well, you can easily remedy that,' Abercrombie said.

'Can I?' he said. 'Can I?' his helplessness, he imagined, only too apparent.

'For one thing, you could have mentioned it in a reasonable tone of voice,' Abercrombie said. He went out into the corridor and began to pick up his boots and his rucksack, and to re-coil his rope. One or two students, smiling, had paused at the door.

And when, finally, Abercrombie had departed, carrying his possessions with him, Coles had moved to the window to fidget, as was his habit, with his briefcase then his books, saying eventually, 'I shouldn't let 'Crombie get under your skin, Colin. It's not worth it.'

'It's the general futility, Arthur,' he said.

'Futility?' Coles moved the word around his mouth. 'Futility of what?'

'Of everything, Arthur.' He was startled himself by the ferocity of his mood.

'Well.' Coles hesitated. He examined him for a while. 'In what way are things so futile, then?' he said.

'In what ways aren't they? In every way.' He spread out his arms to indicate his mood.

'There's your work,' Coles said.

'There is.'

'There's also your family.'

A note of apology had entered Coles's voice.

'There is my wife, there are my children. There is a house, mortgaged yet nevertheless almost mine, a set of parents, in-laws . . . I can count. I can add. I have a certain mathematical ability, Arthur.'

Coles nodded; he trembled slightly: his narrow face and balding head – a thin reef of hair encircling a tall and some-what slender skull – had flushed. 'I'm sorry,' he said, yet for what he didn't seem sure.

'Yes, well. There you are,' he told him.

'I'd like to help,' Coles said, quite suddenly, flushing deeper.

'You think I need help, Arthur?'

8

Coles blinked behind his glasses. 'I don't really know what you're trying to say,' he said.

Pasmore looked away; he looked at the floor and shrugged.

A quietness descended on them both.

After a while Coles said, 'Has something happened?' brushing his hand across his head.

Pasmore didn't reply. His hands now in his pockets he stared back at the floor.

Yet he felt hurt, oddly numbed and frightened when, with a brief, almost violent look, Coles walked quickly out of the room. 'What have I said now?' he asked himself, staring at the door.

He saw Coles later that day, in the afternoon. It was nearly tea-time. He was sitting in a lecture hall, alone, packing his briefcase, preparing to leave for home. The room was warm and stuffy.

'I was thinking, Arthur,' he said. 'Why don't you come home and have some tea? It's years since Kay saw you. We could leave now if you're ready. It won't take us long.'

Perhaps Coles had been avoiding him all day. He took off his glasses and began to clean them.

'Could you ring home?' he said. 'Or leave a message?'

'I don't know,' Coles said. He breathed on the lenses, polishing them with his handkerchief. The skin around his eyes was white, and ringed slightly from the pressure of the frames.

'I'd like you to come,' he said, and added, 'I'm sorry about this morning.'

'Yes,' Coles said. He stood up, gathering his briefcase, then glanced down at his watch. 'How long will it take?'

'About ten minutes. To get there. I shouldn't think much more.'

'I haven't any change,' he said, feeling in his pockets.

'I have some,' he said.

'Well, then,' he said, and looked round, blindly, for a telephone.

A short bus ride took them from the Georgian precincts of the college up the steep hill to Islington. A few minutes' walk from the bus stop, following the upper contour of the ridge, brought them to the square of Victorian houses. The sky, after the day's earlier darkness, had begun to clear, though the trees in the square virtually excluded any sunlight. Despite their white renovated fronts the houses themselves were sunk in shadow. Coles, whose last visit had been late one night, after a college party, looked round freshly at the sight.

'It must be a good investment,' he said, 'the house. I see they're renovating them all now.' His own modest dwelling was south of the river, in Clapham.

'Yes,' Pasmore said. He led the way towards the door, the central one of the southern façade and the one which, as a consequence, stood in the midst of the deepest shadow. A curious mood, one almost of inertia, had overtaken him since climbing off the bus – a feeling which he obviated now by taking out his key and inserting it in the lock. The door, however, was pushed to, apparently accidentally, by an onrush of bodies the other side.

'For Christ's sake,' he said. Then shouting, 'Kay!' he opened the door again, holding it back with his arm to allow Coles, smiling now, to enter.

Kay herself had already appeared at the far end of the passage, the door behind her opening to reveal the large room at the rear – at that moment, as the two men entered, full of sunlight. Her figure, silhouetted, rested there like some slender attenuation of the light itself. Then she called,

'Arthur. I didn't recognize you,' and came down the hall to shake his hand.

'I can't even get in the door,' Pasmore said, his moodiness still that which had preoccupied him outside, a kind of surliness with which he disowned the children as they clung to his legs, demanding to be lifted. He pushed them down, calling out, though neither his tone nor his actions discouraged them in any way and he was obliged more or less to carry them with him to the room at the rear.

This was a fairly large interior put together from two previous rooms. A bay window opened onto the steps which led down to the garden, a lawn with tufted knotted grass circuited by an ash path and a thin, flowerless border. A broad table stood in the alcove formed by the bay; across it was strewn the debris from the children's tea. Several large dolls lay about the room, either on the floor or propped up lugubriously on the chairs like swollen replicas of the children themselves.

Distracted by all this evidence of communal life he was for a moment unaware of a second woman smiling up at him from across the room.

'Colin,' she said. 'How are you?'

'Oh. Marjorie,' he said, his mood now swiftly changing.

Two more children knelt by the chair in which, dressed in a black leather skirt and black leather boots, Marjorie was half-lounging. Neither child looked up but pored over some mechanical puzzle strewn on the floor between them. Only when kicked reproachfully by the toe of Marjorie's swinging boot – one leg laid carelessly and revealingly over the other – did they glance up, half-startled, and frown in acknowledgement at Pasmore, failing to recognize Coles altogether before returning to their task.

'Marjorie, this is Arthur Coles,' he said, and added,

'Arthur, this is Marjorie Newsome, a friend of Kay's from round the corner.'

Coles smiled. He nodded amicably at Marjorie across the room. Uncertain perhaps, for a moment, whether his introduction required a handshake, he gazed genially at her through his black-framed lenses. Then, deciding from Marjorie's leggy indolence that no further gesture was required of him, he turned his smile once more towards the children.

Susan pulled at his arm, tentatively, almost speculatively, shaking back her fair hair, her blue eyes moving up to Kay's as if to measure out the significance of her action.

Cynthia had no such awareness. She hung, literally, on his free hand, her legs curled up, her feet struggling to secure a hold on his knees. He was pulled down by her lithe, wriggling weight, jarred, and pulled down again, and she called out to him, in some odd way tormented.

He turned to her, releasing the other girl to forestall her mood, hoisting her up with two hands, turning her over in his arms, changing the gesture finally into something of an embrace.

Under Coles's smiling scrutiny, however, she began to wriggle, then to kick, and, matching her despair with something of his own, Pasmore put her down. He watched helplessly as she flung herself face down in a chair, weeping. 'Now, love,' he said. 'What is it?'

She buried her head in her arms.

'Leave her,' Kay said. 'I'll see to her.'

'Yes,' he said, and turned away, the boy still holding to his legs.

He clung to him, looking up at Coles, not directly, but shyly, sideways, from beneath deep, frowning brows.

'Hello, little man,' Coles had said, bending slightly, his hands on his knees. 'What's your name?'

12

The boy backed away, sliding behind Pasmore's legs, waiting as he might behind a door, his eyes dark and listening.

'Kenneth,' Pasmore said to Coles with some sort of relief.

'Ah, yes,' Coles said, straightening, uncertain whether to pursue his interest in the boy.

'We'll go next door,' Pasmore said and, detaching himself from this, the last of his children, he led the way back into the passage and into the smaller room which overlooked the shadowed square.

Unlike the varnished floor of the previous interior the floor of this room was carpeted from wall to wall. Furniture of a more slender, less robust design was arranged in spoke-like fashion around the marble fireplace. By the window stood a desk, facing onto the square, its surface occupied by a great number of books, papers, sheets and files, the majority of them arranged in neat, almost obsessively tidy piles.

There was the sound of Coles's voice from the room next door, then of Kay's and Marjorie's laughter, and a moment later Cynthia's crying stopped. When Coles finally came in his face was flushed.

'Oh, work, work, work,' he said, clapping his hands. He gazed round at the room. 'What have we got here?'

He crossed over to the desk and began to glance through the papers. Some he had evidently seen before; over others he gave little sighs and groans.

'When are we going to put some of this stuff together?' he said, shifting one or two piles around.

'I don't know,' Pasmore said. As soon as Coles had disturbed one pile he set it straight. 'I dig it all up. I don't really know what to do with it. You'd think after all this time some sort of idea would come to mind.'

'Yes,' Coles said. He was still stooped to the desk, bowed, his elbows tucked into his sides. He looked superficially, in silhouette, like a bird of prey.

Pasmore stepped back and gazed out of the window.

In the square, several women with prams were collecting round the hut in the gardens. The sunlight, breaking through the leaves, lit up their figures.

'The trouble is, Arthur,' he said, 'having established the nature of other men's immortality, secularly speaking, I'm beginning to feel disturbed that my own will be left to or neglected by the same devices.'

'I'm not too sure,' Coles said, 'that I know what you mean.'

'I mean,' he said, gesturing to the window, 'how will they know, or why should they care, that I've treated my wife well, my children likewise, and that I've worked hard and conscientiously all my life?'

'Well,' Coles said, still gazing at the desk, 'they'll know,' and added, looking up, 'your wife and children.'

'Yes,' he said. 'Nevertheless, it's strange. I've often thought about it, but now I'm beginning to worry about it, the relative anonymity, even in my work, let alone here, of everything I think most significant and precious.'

Then, seeing Coles's look, he turned away.

In the square thin clouds of smoke rose from the women's cigarettes.

'What it amounts to,' he said, 'is that for you morality is a function of the sensibility, whereas for me, brought up in a world of working-class aphorisms, it's a thing of fetishes and customs.'

'I don't think I understand,' Coles said. He was gazing at him with some concern.

'I come from a class of people,' Pasmore said, 'of which,

14

only a hundred years ago, only one in ten survived to the age of thirty. Instincts bred from that don't die out as quickly as you imagine.'

Coles held out his hand, whether in gentle deprecation or not it was impossible, in one so physically unco-ordinated, to tell.

'The only reason I don't lay into every woman I fancy, *any* woman I fancy, Arthur, is a morbid, shattering fear of what would happen if I did. A fear, Arthur, whose proportions I don't think you can even remotely imagine.'

The light glinted off Coles's glasses. 'What would happen,' he said, 'to whom?' He seemed in no way surprised by this confession, turning to him, his hand held to his head.

'To Kay,' Pasmore said. 'To her parents, to my parents, to my children . . . to tribes of people back home who see me as some God-given appeaser of all their private hysterias and doubts. It's not me you see here, Arthur. I'm merely an appendage to a long line of stifled obsessions. The head of a caterpillar so long that if you tried to pull it out of its hole you'd be here from now until . . . well.' He spread out his arms, gazing at Coles with his appeal. 'The situation boils down to one thing, Arthur. How to accommodate adultery within the conventional framework of marriage.'

Coles's smile deepened as if the absurdity of such an assertion only deepened, for him, Pasmore's charm.

'It sounds familiar,' Pasmore added, yet as if what he had just said, as a definition of his ailments, came as something of a surprise if not a shock. 'No doubt in Clapham they have ways of dealing with it.'

Coles hesitated, then said, 'No,' shaking his head.

'I see.' Pasmore watched his friend intently. 'You

15

think I should face up to myself and these things would vanish.'

'Not vanish.' Coles's smile had disappeared.

From the next room came the sound of the children's voices, then of Marjorie's and Kay's.

He glanced out of the window, at the group of women seated by their prams – some knitting, some smoking, the majority of them chatting – as if at that moment not one of them, given the slightest encouragement, be it ever so feeble and tangential, would he have hesitated from assaulting, babies or no babies, prams or no prams, pregnant or not. The weight of his feelings crumbled his spirits. He felt absolutely downcast, glancing back at Coles now with some vague longing for revenge. It was as if in fact Coles had invited some such reaction – so perverted were those means by which, theoretically at least, people should have been able to enter and to leave his life.

'Well,' he said finally, avoiding Coles's gaze altogether, 'I'll have to think that one over, mate.'

A short while later, when Kay brought in their tea, he was packing away the various books and papers and Coles himself was preparing to leave.

Two

Pasmore was a big man; that is, he viewed himself as a big man, though he was one or two inches short of being six feet. He had broad shoulders and heavy legs, bowed it seemed from the weight of bone and muscle. His hair was dark, his eyes dark, too, and though this darkness gave him a somewhat melancholic look, the eyes themselves were set in a roundish, high-cheeked, even brightish face, full-lipped, almost pugnacious, with a jutting brow, his figure not unlike that of a wrestler's tensing to a fall.

His wife was of an altogether slighter build, fair-haired, blue-eyed, slim-featured, delicately boned; she had about her a startled, apprehensive look, the eyes bright, gleaming, like those of an animal peering from its burrow. About them both, at first sight, there was a feeling of self-division.

Pasmore was almost thirty. His wife was two years younger. They had met at college and had married one year later after Pasmore was finally settled in his job. The area in which they had chosen to live had previously been occupied by working-class families. The houses themselves had been quite small, formless, almost without shape. Now most of them had been restored. White, gleaming fronts confronted each other across narrow streets, or, in the case of the square, overlooked the cultivated patch of the central gardens. The sun shone most frequently into the rear windows of the house, into the large living area and the tiny garden, and into the Pasmores' bedroom on the floor above. At the front the two small rooms given over to the children looked out directly to the massive, coiling branches of the plane trees which stood like columns around the perimeter of the narrow square.

From the roof of the house – which, in the past, Pasmore had spent much of his spare time renovating – it was possible to see the roofs of the college buildings clustered amongst those of Bloomsbury below, and, further off, in the evening, the lights which lit up the sky in an orange sheen above the West End.

They had lived in the house for several years. In it, for most of that time, they had both been happy; in it their children had been born, in it they had celebrated their successes and consoled each other over their various defeats: only recently, it seemed, had anything gone wrong.

For some time – for longer, in fact, than he cared to remember – Pasmore had been troubled by his dreams; and of all his dreams, by one in particular. He was running in a race, not unlike those races he had run, stoically though with no great enterprise, at school, when he had begun to be overtaken not merely by the runners but by all those idlers and dullards who jogged, or even walked along at the rear. Quite soon, despite all his efforts, he'd been left behind; each time he woke up with a sense of terror.

Kay herself could see nothing frightening in the dream at all. 'But it's not just the feeling,' he told her, 'of being passed that I find so awful, so much as the feeling that, despite being last, I don't want the race itself to finish. I know it sounds ridiculous. And I suppose in a sense it can even be explained. But what I can't understand, despite the triviality of the dream, is its undiminishing sense of terror.'

Then, invariably, seeing her expression, he would laugh at his own misgivings and turn away.

Of only one thing in his life had he ever been ashamed – at least to the extent of admitting it to himself – and that was his job. He had continued at college, as a teacher, principally to prolong a situation he was used to, in which no definite decisions had to be taken, and in which, initially, he had further time to think things over and decide what he really wanted to do. From the age of five his life had been spent in one educational institution after another, dourly and stubbornly at first – his parents, as he'd indicated to Coles, were relatively poor and his work had been his only credential – then more pleasantly and triumphantly later when his efforts, in one sinecure or another, had begun to pay off. Now, however, he was coming to a point where he'd begun to sense that all his efforts had been in vain. He had applied for a fellowship – and much to his surprise had been awarded it – and had, somewhat belatedly, begun to write a book – his subject was the lives of certain evangelical idealists who had lived in the industrial north of England in the early part of the nineteenth century, a part of the country, if not a temperament, with which from childhood he had been familiar – and yet, before either of these events could in any sense be said to have been consolidated he had begun to realize that the missing elements of his existence were not to be identified in any of these terms, either of his work, that is, or of his private life. Where else he could look, and for what, he had no idea.

He had few friends. In fact, when he looked round and tried to imagine what real friendship must be like, he decided he had no friends at all. 'Look, no friends', was a qualification of his independence, as well as an expression of a certain inalienable right to feel that, in their hearts, no one really knew him at all. He had been, and still was, a good and faithful husband; he had been, as it happened, a good and faithful teacher – and to his parents, still living, a good and certainly faithful son. Where had all this faith and goodness got him? It was as if the tenets by which life had been judged and settled in the past had melted into nothing. Was history – was life itself – really in such a mess?

One of his difficulties was that the strength of his constitution worked so robustly against his obsessions. He was, he knew, a secure person. He encountered all the hazards of life from a firm sense of his own and other people's reality. It was this which, in his own life, had created such a curious paradox; for it seemed to him that because of this security, this innate sense of the reliability of natural processes, their substantiality and permanence, he was excluded from much if not all the relevant and meaningful experiences of his time. Here he was, set down in – of all things – an era of disintegration, a period in which there was a complete disruption of those processes which in him were (as far as he could tell) so wholesomely integrated. Almost furtively, and with decreasing resistance, he had begun to see how everything that was good in his life, his peace of mind, his modesty, his reliability, his self-effacement, even his sense of achievement, was irrelevant to the kind of life which he felt obliged to live. How meaningful was his existence if he could not transpose himself into the world of individuals whose experience, patently, all around him, was lacking in those self-validating certainties which made up all he knew of himself as an individual?

He was reluctant – driven to the other extreme – to measure out his world in deficiencies: deficiencies prejudicial, that is, to his moral well-being. He could, as many had, decide that his times were empty of the real food of his aspirations – hopeless, viewless, helpless, lacking that centre of credibility from which, at one time, all things had seemed to stem and to which all things had returned. To have accepted and believed all this would have left him on the side of those people he despised most; those who, amongst other things, looked to the past – or even the future – for the reassurance lacking in the present. He had to be content, it seemed, with a certain pride, if not a certain degree of self-pity, his consolation coming from feeling extraneous, self-tortured, lonely and confused.

As the last days of the summer term passed, he began to regret having confided in Coles. He watched his friend go away on holiday – he was taking his family, his wife and two children, camping as he did each year – without, relatively, another word having passed between them. He couldn't help but feel betrayed.

Left on his own over the summer months he began to suspect – it was nothing unusual: the very conventionality of the idea, in one sense, predisposed him towards it – that he was going insane. It affected everything around him. He found, for one thing, he was unable to touch his wife. It was odd; he felt neither repelled nor attracted by Kay; it was an inability to touch her, as simple as that; so that at times, lying in bed, she would – under what circumstances could he have revealed it to Coles? – begin to stroke herself in those places reserved, he had thought, solely for his caresses; stroking herself, that is, despairingly, reproach-fully, until, provoking some cry of agitation from him, she would say, 'If you don't, somebody's got to,' drawing her head away with a kind of disgust, completely distracted, her voice so unlike Kay's, her actions for that matter so unlike Kay's, that he scarcely recognized her. 'Why won't you? Why won't you?' she would ask.

Although it didn't happen very often he worried about it a great deal. The more he worried about it the more uncommunicative he became. Like Kay herself, though reflective even introspective by nature, he wasn't a person given by temperament to self-enquiry. His natural tendency, once his capacity for hard work was exhausted, was to wait and see. Even now he couldn't help but think that, whatever his present circumstances, the outcome would inevitably be for the good. The gloom was only there to emphasize the light. He only thought he was going mad during those moments when his distractions could find no other relief.

He still loved Kay, he was sure. Although unable to touch her, or to communicate with her, now he came to think of it, in any way whatsoever, he knew the moment she was out of the house his thoughts would turn to her, wondering where she was, trying to imagine what she was doing; so that if, say, she were a little late in returning he immediately began to worry, growing, as the time passed, almost distracted, looking out of windows, going to the door, even to the street corner, to anticipate her arrival. His anxiety was so near the surface it could do nothing but reassure him.

Yet plainly something was wrong. On certain mornings he would waken beside her to be immediately aware of the tension, like waking to a room on fire, to flames and smoke. The whole place was alive with the vibrancy of the figure beside him. His body ached. If he had given in and touched her he was sure he would have cried out, in rage, in grief, in some peculiar and wholly unimaginable torment. He couldn't understand it. He was oppressed.

Towards the end of the summer they went away on holiday. They took the children to the coast. The land was flat, the beach broad and empty. It was almost the beginning of October.

He went out a great deal on his own, walking on the sands. It was possible to walk a mile or two miles in either direction without meeting a soul. It was cold and quiet, in the evenings very misty, the sun setting down the coast where the land and the sea met.

The children too were quiet, subdued, suddenly aware, now they were on their own, of a peculiar inertia. He would come across them in odd corners of the hotel crying, unable to give any explanation. He talked to Kay, yet very little came out of it. He resented having to acknowledge her at all.

One day a dog appeared on the beach. He threw a stick for it into the sea, watching the dog flounder through the shallow waves and eventually, dutifully, bring it back.

It appeared the next day, and the next, walking behind him as he strolled along the beach, away from the hotel, towards the low headland which he invariably set as his destination. He whistled to it, and even gave it a name. Occasionally, in the evenings, the owner of the hotel had to drive it from the door.

'Why don't you play with the children?' Kay said. 'Instead of the dog.'

'I don't know,' he told her.

'I suppose because it makes no demands.'

'That's right,' he said.

There was very little now that passed between them.

On the last night of their holiday there was a gale. Kay had already fallen asleep when he first heard it. He got up and dressed, glanced in at the children, then went down to the beach.

The place was a howling immensity. Great, thrashing bulwarks of water streamed in with tumbling, broken crests, fanning out over the hard sand. The sea had risen, covering the beach where previously he had been walking. Banks of shingle and debris had already been flung up, mounds of weed, fractured beams and stacks of large, whitish stone. The air shuddered to the movement of the waves, visible far out, the white spume glowing, and flooding in from the darkness.

He gazed out towards the sea, shaken, as if some segment of his life had been dislodged and was floating off, like an island. He felt like calling out, screaming. He pulled up his collar and went back to the hotel.

For some time he sat behind the shaking windows, staring out at the darkness and the sea.

The following morning the storm had subsided. At the station the dog appeared on the platform: it had followed the taxi the short distance from the hotel. He sat watching it from inside the carriage. It stood looking up, barking, wagging its tail.

The train started. One of the children leaned out of the window. Beyond the child's head Pasmore glimpsed the sea: a barrier of fir trees beyond which the long breakers rolled smoothly in to the beach.

After a while downland rose on either side and a little later the train pulled into a town.

The Autumn term began. Coles, considerably tanned from his life in the open air, treated him with the same coolness. He tried to examine what had happened between them but could see nothing to justify his friend's aloofness. He looked round at the children, at Kay, at the house which, in the past, he had spent so much of his time renovating and repairing, and wondered what it was in all this that was somehow misshapen. He felt a kind of fury gaining momentum inside him, yet at what he couldn't be sure.

One night Kay woke him from his sleep.

She was leaning over him, one arm on his shoulder. 'Are you all right?' she said.

He waited, uncertain.

'Are you all right?' she asked him again.

'Yes,' he said. 'What is it?'

Without waiting to be reassured she released him and turned over on her side.

A few nights later she woke him again. It happened more frequently. On each occasion she said nothing, merely nudging his back or shaking his shoulder. 'What's the matter?' he asked her.

'You were talking,' she said.

Yet, a few nights later, he heard the sound himself. It was a kind of moaning, a whimpered sound, like an animal caught in a trap. He struggled to wake, assuming it was one of the children. His mouth was open; tears streamed from his eyes.

Kay had mounded the blankets round her head.

The following morning, aware of some new mood, she asked him what had happened. 'What is it?' she said. 'What's going on?'

'I don't know,' he said. He watched her intently. 'Something's the matter. I don't know what it is.'

'To do with me?'

'I don't know.'

'It must be.'

After a while he said, 'Yes. I think it is.'

That evening, when he came home and the children had

gone to bed, he said, 'I think it's better, you know, that I leave you.'

She scarcely raised her head.

'If only for a while,' he told her.

'Why?' she said.

'I don't know how to explain it.'

She shook her head.

'Nevertheless,' he said, 'I think it's better.'

'If that's what you want,' she said.

'It's not what I want,' he said. 'I just feel I haven't any choice.'

Later that night she said, 'Why don't you talk about it if I'm to blame?'

He had never seen her so distressed. The fear it aroused only drove him on.

'There's nothing more to say,' he told her.

She watched him with a kind of horror. 'What is it?' she said. 'How can it suddenly be like this if it's been good and we've been happy so long?'

'I don't know what it is,' he said.

She shook her head, crying.

'Haven't you any feeling left for me at all?'

'No,' he said. 'I haven't.'

'Well, then,' she said. 'You'd better go.'

And yet, looking round for a room came as something of a shock, and not merely the price – for he certainly couldn't afford to run another establishment – but the whole world of living in single rooms and flats to which he was suddenly exposed: tiny garrets, rooms at the tops of small hotels, rooms in houses which had long forgotten the meaning of life, of family life, as he knew it. It was like lifting up floorboards and finding nothing but ruin: the self-containment, the cramming into a single space of all the utensils necessary for one person's existence; a fire, a basin, a cooker, a bed, a chair; it was worse than prison for it pretended to some sort of freedom. It was a kind of hell.

He found, as he had begun to suspect, that there was no going back: he had lived in such rooms as a student. Neither, it seemed, was there any going forward. He didn't know what to do. He no longer knew what he felt. He saw nothing but confusion. He turned his attention increasingly on Kay.

He began to watch her like an executioner; cold, practical, a role thrust upon him out of nowhere. He watched her for faults that might reassure him, certain physical defects, animosity, hatred, contempt. All he saw, however, was her bewilderment. Like him, she didn't know what to do nor what to feel because she didn't know what had happened. Here was a decent home, a respectable marriage, broken in two for no reason at all.

'The house, decorating it, everything,' he said, 'was just to hide the rot. Blind us to it.'

Yet he had felt so happy and pleased restoring the house: even now he tended to look round at it with a certain nostalgia for faults that might be corrected.

'Why don't you leave?' she said. 'Anything's better than this.' It was this threat he held over her, hoping she might crumble.

'When I find a room I will,' he told her as though the suitability of such a room, when it was found, was important to them both.

Yet he had given up searching. He still glanced at the accommodation board in the college, but never followed up the addresses.

'What is the matter?' she asked him again.

'Isn't it obvious enough?' He grew wild at his helplessness. 'Whatever there was has vanished.'

'Does it go as easily as that?'

'It comes as easily. It goes as easily. There's no need to go looking for precedents.'

'And that makes everything else futile as well?'

'You don't believe it?'

'No,' she said. 'I don't believe it.' She refused to cry.

'It's because you don't want to.'

'No. I don't,' she told him.

And because he waited and hung around, demanding that she crumble, her hopes began to rise. It was dreadful. He was locked in on every side.

Even Coles was affected. His look, almost imperceptibly, had grown into one of condolence, those suspended feelings with which one watches a fatal illness, helpless oneself, a little deranged by the futility: the look of someone who, even had they wished it, could think of nothing to do or say.

His helplessness turned to fury. The entire house shrank in gloom. In order to justify his situation he began to devour the children. No sooner was he in the house than the tyranny began.

The sensation of inertia mounted, the opposite to hysteria, some considerable distance from resignation, an indefinable, raging immobility imposed, he could not help feeling, not from within but without. His life seemed cancelled out by a series of endless contradictions. He loved Kay, yet he couldn't bear to be near her. He loved his children, yet their existence numbed him to the bone.

Three

He shared a course of evening lectures with Coles and Abercrombie. It had, as its general title, 'Portraits from the Past': his own contributions were drawn from the Commonwealth, Coles's from the Restoration, Abercrombie's from the Industrial Revolution. Their audiences were comprised of elderly men, middle-aged women, several youths and a group of nuns.

One evening his attention had been caught by a face smiling across at him from the bank of listening heads, a look almost of ridicule if not abuse as if it had found in what he was saying, or in the manner in which it was expressed, something absurd if not grotesque.

The face was that of a woman in her late thirties, a vague, rather anonymous figure sitting high up in the theatre, to one side of the audience.

The following week he noticed her arrival. Her look was cold and austere, almost frightening. She wore a belted coat; her head was bare. She had sharp and very clear features.

On other evenings, quite fortuitously, he would catch her eye. He learned to recognize her looks. '*This man is a fool*', '*This woman likewise*', were conveyed by a slight pulling down of the corner of her mouth. A raised brow indicated some form of appreciation, a fixed smile some sort of disfavour. A rather tense expression, her eyes glazed and wide open, indicated, if not boredom, at least a certain disbelief.

A turning away of the head, glancing down, came whenever some point had been recognized, or she were pleased. Over everything hung an incredible aloofness.

One day he met her in the college. He was crossing the yard from the wing of the college when he saw her walking away from the office towards a large car parked in the centre of the area where as a rule no cars were allowed at all.

A chauffeur was arguing with the beadle, a tall, red-faced man in a tall hat and a purple, gold-brocaded suit.

'Is this a friend of yours, Mr Pasmore?' the beadle said when he tried to intervene.

'It is, yes,' he said, glancing at the chauffeur. He too was in uniform, virtually anonymous, however, but for the shiny neb of his cap.

'The parking of vehicles, sir,' he said, 'isn't allowed in this part of the quad.'

'Quad' was said with a certain affectation: more usually it was referred to as the yard.

'It won't happen again, Jim,' he said.

'Harry,' the beadle said and walked slowly away, pulling on his gloves.

'I'm sorry,' she said as if this incident alone had brought him back to mind. She looked up at him, then at the buildings.

'Is there anything I can do to help?' he said.

'Well,' she said. She shook her head.

She was dressed in a dark blue coat.

Its collar ran out directly from under her dark hair and was fastened by a single button at her throat. The darkness and sobriety seemed habitual, like someone in mourning. She had no hat.

'You've caught me, I'm afraid, in the midst of changing courses.'

30

She held up several leaflets in her gloved hand.

From a nearby window several students had begun to whistle, not at him, he suspected, nor at her, but at the idea of a chauffered limousine in the precincts of the college.

'You wouldn't recommend them?' she said.

'Well.' He maintained a proprietorial air, glancing at the window.

'What would you recommend?' she said.

'For popularity, or interest?'

'Both.'

She looked back at him directly.

'I don't know,' he said. 'Probably nothing you could get in this place.'

She examined him a moment longer then turned to the car. The rear door was already open. 'Well, thank you again,' she said, 'for interceding with the beadle.'

'Any time,' he said and stepped away.

The door was closed. For a moment he stood gazing in at her.

Then the car slid away.

It scarcely made a sound. It negotiated the ranks of parked family saloons and tiny student roadsters and turned, past the beadle's lodge, into the busy street outside.

One evening he saw her emerging from the college building. Behind her walked three nuns, their cowls glistening in the lamplight. A slow procession of people trailed across the yard to the gates. At first he assumed she had seen him: she crossed directly towards him only to pause by a small car and open the door.

She glanced up at the sound of his steps on the gravel.

'Hello,' he said. He sounded immensely cheerful, some genial guardian of the place she couldn't help disturbing. 'How's it going?'

'All right,' she said.

'Come for a drink.'

He saw the look of surprise, if not annoyance, then the hesitation: it was contained in a single movement. She opened the door of the car a little further and threw in several books. 'All right,' she said. 'Is it far?'

He shook his head. 'Just to the corner.'

She began to walk off then as if no invitation had been given. Her heels dragged slightly in the gravel.

'How are the lectures?' he asked her. He had to walk quickly to catch her up.

'Not very interesting.'

'What were you hoping for?' he said.

'Oh . . .' She shrugged, glancing up as they reached the street. He indicated the way and, as they crossed over, wondered whether he might take her arm.

There was little traffic.

'You can't expect a great deal of enlightenment,' he said, 'for thirty pence a term.'

'The fee's a pound,' she said with no expression at all.

The bar was almost empty.

She went to a table and sat down.

As he carried the drinks back he glanced up at her directly.

She was gazing abstractly before her. Her eyes were set in a slight frown. As he set the glasses down she glanced round at the bar.

'Do you come here often?'

'No,' he said.

She nodded, took her drink, sipped it then put it down.

A moment later she picked it up again and finished it completely.

'Let me get you another,' he said.

'I'll get it.'

She caught the barman's eye and signalled him over. There was a certain briskness about her now. She gave the order with an upward, open, half-seductive look, as quickly retracted as it was presented, her eyes momentarily alight.

He indicated the college. 'Perhaps you're not cut out for this kind of life.'

'No,' she said, 'perhaps not.' And a moment later added, 'I don't know. You can't be sure.'

She opened her handbag, a small, sling-like case, and took out a cigarette. 'Would you like one?'

'I don't smoke,' he said.

She nodded as if this were very much what she had suspected. 'Do you mind?'

The small silver lighter – its design corresponding in some way with the case – she propped for a moment before her face, flicked it and dipped the cigarette into the flame. 'How long have you been teaching?' she said.

'Oh,' he said. 'For quite a while.'

The tray was laid on the table before them; as he removed the two glasses she cut off the tip from the change and poured the coins into her bag. A tiny clasp secured it. 'Are you married?'

'Yes,' he said.

She laid her bag beside the glass.

'And you?'

'Yes.' Her voice was drained of any interest. She held the cigarette before her, gazing down. 'Have you been working this evening?' she said.

'Yes.'

33

He added, 'I leave here though, next term.'

'Where will you be going?'

She half-smiled. Her mouth was drawn back at one corner. She blew out a cloud of smoke which drifted slowly past his head.

'I have a fellowship.'

'What's that?'

'A year off.'

'To do what?'

'To put some work together.' He added, 'At least, that's the intention.'

'It sounds very nice.' A certain malevolence, he thought, had come into her voice. 'I didn't know you could do that sort of thing.'

'You can't.'

'I see.'

'This is American money. I've been trying to get it for some time.' He laughed; she continued to regard him aloofly. 'For that you get special dispensation. A term off. In this instance, three.'

'Perhaps they won't know,' she said, 'what to do without you.'

'Didn't you like my lectures? he said.

She shook her head.

'Why not?'

'I don't know.' She held her fingers against her forehead. 'No, I didn't like them, I suppose,' she said.

He began to smile.

'Have another drink,' he said.

'A last one. Then I must be going.'

It took a little time to catch the barman's eye.

'I didn't think,' she said, 'that they meant a great deal to you, either.'

34

'I'm surprised you noticed.'

'I notice quite a few things,' she said.

He didn't catch the tone precisely.

The bar turned generally to watch her departure.

'I'll walk with you to the car,' he said when he realized she expected to be left outside. She had put out her hand to say goodbye.

'Really, there's no need,' she said.

But she had already turned towards the college. She walked with her hands in her coat pockets, the bag hanging from her wrist.

'What will you do about your lectures?' he said.

'Drop them.'

It might have sounded too much like a comment on their encounter, for she added after a moment, 'Probably. I don't know. I'm not sure.'

They walked the rest of the way in silence.

'Good-night, then,' she said when they reached the college gates. She held out her hand again.

'I never learned your name,' he said.

'Helen.'

He watched her walk past the beadle's lodge to her car. It stood alone now in the yard. In the lodge itself the beadle, hatless, was reading an evening paper.

As he walked down the street to the bus stop she passed him in the car.

They met a week later, whether by accident or design he couldn't tell. She was coming out of the same lecture theatre: he happened to be passing.

'You're still here, then?' he said.

For a moment she seemed surprised, uncertain who he was.

35

'Have you got half an hour?' he said. 'I'm just knocking off.'

'I don't know.' She asked him the time.

For a moment, together, they gazed up at the clock over the beadle's lodge. The three nuns walked slowly past and disappeared into the darkness of the street outside.

Her car wasn't in the yard.

'Do we have to go to the same place?' she said.

'No.' He shook his head.

She looked up again at the clock and said, 'All right, then. Half an hour.'

She walked along then quite casually, her hands in her pockets.

'How was this evening?' he said.

'Oh.' She shook her head. It was as if he were someone else entirely.

For a while they walked along in silence.

'How about this place?' he said when they'd gone some distance from the college.

She scarcely glanced up. From her pocket she produced a scarf and tied it round her head. She looked neither at the people nor the interior, simply going to an empty table and sitting down.

He asked for the drinks to be brought over.

'Do they know you here?' she said.

He shook his head, looking round. 'I've never been here in my life.'

She wore no make-up. Her eyes were wide, a little startled.

From her pocket she took the same cigarette case and the same lighter, offering him one, closing her eyes at his refusal and taking one herself. 'What are you smiling at?' she said.

36

'I'm astonished you're here,' he said.

'Yes.' She smiled herself.

'Do you have many friends?' he asked her.

She suddenly laughed. The dark eyes examined him in surprise.

'What does your husband do?' he said.

'He works,' she said. 'Like any other.'

'This,' he said, and gestured at the room, 'he wouldn't approve of.'

'I don't know.' She shrugged. 'He'd probably feel very flattered.'

'Knowing you were here?'

'Any precautions I might take,' she said, 'are entirely for my own convenience.'

He wasn't sure what she meant. He said, 'I see.'

She added, 'Would you like another drink?'

She waited for him to signal the barman. 'And you,' she said. 'What does your wife do?'

'I imagine very much the same as you.'

'Oh, I don't know,' she said. 'I'm very lazy.' She watched him a moment, still smiling, then added, 'How many children have you got?'

'Three.'

She laid a note on the table and waited for the barman to put out the change. He collected it for her from the tray.

'I've two,' she said.

'I suppose you find all this a bit preposterous.'

'What?'

'These demands.' He wasn't sure.

'Oh. Demands are always preposterous,' she said.

She leaned her head on her hand, her cigarette smoking by her cheek. Her eyes, above her couched cheek, were half-closed.

37

For a while she said nothing. Then she added, 'Everything, I suppose, has its own kind of form.'

'Yes?' he said, and added, 'And this?'

'I don't know. The form reveals itself, I imagine, as it goes along.'

'Nevertheless, it is a little strange.'

'Yes,' she said.

They had a third drink then, as on the previous occasion, she decided, without consulting anything, that it was time to go.

'I never asked you,' he said as they walked back through the darkened streets, 'where you live.'

She glanced up. 'Does it matter?'

'No.' He shook his head.

She walked with her arms held to her sides.

He recognized the car eventually, parked in a side-street near the college.

'Shall I see you again?' he said.

'I don't know.'

He gazed at her with much the same sort of coldness.

'If you like.' After a moment she added, 'If you think it's worth it.'

'Where?' he said.

'I've no idea.' She glanced over at the car then back down the street towards the college. 'The same place,' she said, and added, 'You might think of somewhere else to go.'

'I will.'

'Do you want a lift?'

He was about to accept.

For some reason he shook his head. 'I'll walk,' he said.

She got into the car without another word, switched on the lights, then the engine, waved and drove quickly off.

He felt a great sense of relief.

When he reached home he embraced Kay and said, 'Really, things will be all right after all.'

He held her as if he'd returned from a long absence, stunned, a little overwhelmed.

'Goodness,' she said. 'What's happened?'

'Oh.' He shook his head.

Later, he said, 'Surely, at some point, everyone throws up their hands at what they've become.'

'I don't know,' she said. 'I never have.'

'You always have the children.'

'Do they help?'

He didn't answer. She didn't press too closely. It was too strange to go into.

'You seemed to think everything had fallen to pieces,' she said later. 'That there wasn't any chance.'

'Everything was shut in,' he said.

'And now?'

'Everything seems different.'

'Well.' She still watched him in surprise.

The coldness melted. They came alive. She was suddenly very happy.

They went out to the theatre one evening. They scarcely went at all. It seemed part of this invisible event, as if he were entertaining her with the secret, opening the door so that she might see inside.

The house grew in size. The children were restored to favour.

A week later he told her he would be late home in the evening.

'You're usually late,' she said.

'Not to worry,' he told her. 'If I'm late I'll be working in the library.'

39

She spread out her arms. 'Well, all right,' she said, and smiled.

He saw her some little distance off, waiting in the shadow of the office buildings across the street from the beadle's lodge. An odd malignancy had crept into their encounter as if, somewhere, a light had been put out.

'How are you?' he said, and shook her hand.

The same formality was evident in her too, like the moment when he had last seen her. No other intimacy intruded.

'I wasn't sure you'd be here,' he said.

'Yes,' she said. 'I nearly left a message at the college.'

He glanced across at the beadle's lodge, filled suddenly with a kind of dread.

'Have you thought of where we can go?' she said.

'A pub seems the only place. I mean, how well are you known? We could go for a meal. Or a walk.'

She said nothing. Her expression conveyed nothing, neither disappointment nor unease, nor, it seemed, much hope either. It was cold, almost winter. 'In any case,' he said, 'it might be wiser to meet somewhere else. The term ends in a week or so. Things might be easier.'

'Let's go for a drink,' she said, and turned off down the street.

She wore the same scarf as before, the same dark coat, belted. It was like a uniform: the thing she became the moment she slipped it on. In it he saw no desire to please; no desire, even, to please or reassure herself. It was a kind of negation.

She chose once again a corner of the pub, sitting with her back to the other people and gazing not at him but blankly at the wall beyond.

'Aren't you well this evening?' he asked her.

'I'm perfectly all right,' she said. 'Why do you ask?'

He didn't answer, but looked away.

'I suppose all this is a bit absurd.'

'Yes,' he said.

'Perhaps we'd better call a halt.'

'Why don't we get a room?' he said.

The same calmness persisted.

She began to smile.

After a moment she said, 'All right,' and in much the same tone as before added, 'If you think it's worth it.'

Her expression didn't change. She seemed neither surprised nor concerned as if the whole thing had been decided behind her back, by people they didn't know and had never mentioned.

'I can't stay long,' she said. 'Another drink and I'll have to go.'

They sat for the rest of the time in silence.

In a mirror by the bar he saw their reflection: they were like two figures waiting in a station, at a roadside. Like refugees.

In the same silence they got up. In the same silence they walked through the streets.

'How can I get in touch?' he said when they reached the car.

'Perhaps you could leave a message,' she said. 'At the college.'

'It's a little difficult.'

'Well.' She glanced up, frowning, as if she couldn't understand his concern.

'I suppose I could arrange it.'

'Fine,' she said.

'I'll leave it at the lodge.'

41

'Good.'

She got into the car.

'It'll be all right,' he said with some strange ambition to reassure her.

'Oh, I'm sure,' she said and waited for him to close the door.

She waved briefly as she drove away.

He felt curiously dejected.

'You didn't work so late after all,' Kay told him.

'I couldn't wait,' he said, 'to get back home to you.'

In a way it was true: he was so relieved to see her.

He was still feeling very dazed.

The next week he spent all his spare time searching for a room. Many were left vacant by students returning home for Christmas. In this way he discovered a small flat a short distance from the college.

It had two rooms. They comprised the second floor of a small Victorian house, one of a terrace which, on the ground floor, had been converted into shops. The street itself was a shopping arcade, crowded throughout the day and brightly illuminated at night.

The main room looked out onto the stalls, the crowds and the traffic: it was this, primarily, that attracted him to it. A double divan, a gas fire, two armchairs, a cupboard and a table comprised its main furniture. The second, smaller room, across a narrow landing, was equipped as a kitchen. Its single window overlooked a block of tenements and, below, a concrete yard full of parked cars.

The place had a strange intimacy. It came from the feeling of being both in the street and yet above it, looking down on all those heads, on all that activity and traffic.

In the evenings, when the stalls had been wheeled away, an army of scavengers appeared. He had never seen anything like it. At one end of the street a group of men would arrive with brushes and shovels, at the other a larger group, many of them dishevelled, limping and shuffling, picking their way through the mounds of rubbish. Some of them maimed, the majority of them disfigured, they sorted out the remains into paper bags, quarrelling briefly as the two groups converged then, just as quickly, disappearing. A little later, when the lamps came on, a water-cart would arrive and flush the last debris from the gutters. The last thing at night the street would stand empty, glistening, the pavements and the roadway damp and bare.

She came to the flat a few days before Christmas.

He arrived an hour before her, lit the gas fire, tidied the room, brushed the floor, and set a bunch of flowers on the table in the main room.

The bell in the street didn't work. He knelt on the bed, leaning out of the window, watching for her amongst the crowds. The air was full of the cries of the vendors, of the shuffling of hundreds of feet, of the bleating of the traffic pushing its way between the stalls.

He saw her some way off.

She wore a black hat which shielded her face, and a black, astrakhan coat. A small brooch, at first he thought a flower, was pinned near her collar. She was looking up, without any curiosity, at the street numbers.

He went down and waited for her in the doorway. She was still a little distance off, unaware, jostled slightly by the crowd, glancing up at the doors, about her the same incredible aloofness.

When finally she saw him she came forward quite casually, raising her head slightly but scarcely glancing at the building. 'The bell doesn't work,' he said. 'I thought I'd come down.'

'Is this the place?' she said.

He nodded and without any comment she walked inside, down the narrow hallway, pausing in the comparative darkness to make sure of the stairs.

He climbed slowly behind her. The stairs were steep and sharply curved: she found her step with some difficulty, stumbling once, his hand rushing out, brushing her shoe. 'It's all right,' she said and continued up without his help.

When they reached the second landing he stepped before her to open the door.

She came into the room slowly, looking round.

'What do you think?' he said.

She glanced up at him directly, coming to stop in the centre of the room.

'It's somewhere,' he said.

'Yes.'

'You don't like it?'

She took off her hat, bowing her head slightly to one side to draw it off. Then she shook her head, sweeping back her hair.

'It's fine.'

'You don't mind it?'

She glanced round for somewhere to put her hat, laying it eventually on the table beside the flowers.

'It's exactly,' she said, 'as I imagined.'

'Home from home.'

'Absolutely.'

Then she laughed.

She had gone to the window and glanced out. He

44

couldn't see her expression. The sound of her laughter was like that of some other presence, derisive, looking in from outside.

'I don't know,' she said. 'It's like another planet.'

She glanced back at him. Perhaps she was disappointed.

'There's a kitchen as well,' he said, 'across the landing.' He explained the few amenities. 'We're on the phone.'

The telephone stood on a pile of directories on the floor.

'Have we anything in to drink?' she said.

'No.' It was the one thing he'd forgotten.

'It doesn't matter.'

She took off her coat.

He took it from her, scarcely glancing at her, searching for somewhere to put it.

He took it to the wardrobe.

'I don't think,' she said, 'in there.'

He looked round again, found a peg at the back of the door, and hung it up.

She was wearing a black dress, flared slightly from the waist and with buttoned sleeves.

'Well,' she said. 'We're here.'

She took a cigarette from her bag and lit it with the small lighter, then moved over to the fire and stood by it, stroking her arms.

'Well,' she said, looking up. 'How are you?'

'We could look somewhere else,' he said.

'It's fine,' she said. She shook her head. 'I'll give you my share of the rent.'

'That's all right.'

'Is this all the heating there is?'

'Yes,' he said.

She turned back and gazed at the fire, her arms folded, the cigarette held from her.

45

He watched her for some time in silence.

She looked up finally at the wall in front of her, glanced round for somewhere to stub her cigarette, then dropped it in the hearth.

When he hesitated she turned round and slowly raised her arms.

'Are you all right?' she said, smiling.

There was the same look of insolence, almost violent.

Just as quickly it disappeared.

She went to the door, sprang the lock and bolted it.

In some real way this wasn't what he had intended. His arms shook. His legs scarcely held him.

When he closed the curtains the room was illuminated solely by the fire.

Four

It was to Coles that he most wanted to confess it.

He rang him at home one evening – the college was no longer in session – and met him for a drink. At the last moment he hesitated from revealing anything directly, merely insinuating by his exuberance that something astonishing had happened which raised him beyond the level to which at one time he had felt himself to be irretrievably condemned.

Coles watched him with a smile.

'What are you doing for Christmas?' had been his reply.

And yet, if not directly, it was with Coles and with Kay that he celebrated his new-found freedom, the sense of liberation which, once he was away from the room, came pouring out.

There, everything was dark and serious.

The first week they met at the flat every day. There was a blind, almost malicious intensity about their encounters. Only when he left did he feel his spirits rise. Each time he reached home he greeted Kay with a long embrace.

Going to the flat during the day or, if he could invent an excuse, in the evening, he saw Helen each time with a fresh shock of recognition, of suspicion and disbelief. With her his feelings were never still. They ran up against one another, erupting and breaking. Nothing, while he was with her, could rid him of this feeling, a kind of fear. He

47

could never look at her directly. He was most aware of her when she was some distance away, in the darkness, moving towards him or across the room.

Once he was exhausted he could never lie near her.

He got up, made some tea in the kitchen, gazing out at the tenement opposite and the rows of parked cars below.

Occasionally a face would peer out from one of the windows, glance out, sometimes at the sky, then vanish.

She was always remote.

Between leaving her in the bed and her appearing fully dressed he never really looked at her. Once she was dressed he would stand across the room admiring her, aware of his pleasure in watching her come and go.

He learned very little about her. The less he knew the easier he felt.

'I suppose your husband knows nothing of this arrangement?' he asked her.

'I shouldn't think so.'

'Doesn't he think it strange, you going out?'

'He's never there,' she said.

'What time does he go to work on a morning?'

'It varies.'

'And coming back?'

She shrugged. 'Much the same.'

During these examinations she would be lying on her back, smoking, submitting to his questions with a vague air of irritation. He learned not to enquire too directly, nor too deeply. In a way they were both content.

'I've never once heard you use my name,' she told him one morning as, separately, they were about to leave.

He shook his head.

'Perhaps you don't like it.'

'I think I do.'

48

'Or perhaps you've forgotten it.'

He shook his head.

'Well, then . . .' She waited.

'Helen,' he said.

'That's better,' she said and, laughing, kissed his cheek.

Shortly after Christmas Kay's parents arrived.

His father-in-law was a country doctor, stout, white-haired, with a red face and bluish eyes, self-amused, quiet, self-effacing. The mother too was quiet, modest, open-faced: they drew back slightly at the sudden strength of his affection. 'Well, no one's been quite so glad to see me,' the mother said, 'for such a long time.'

She wasn't sure, quite, what to make of his embrace.

There was a certain ruthlessness in him they might have recognized from the start, a certain clumsiness, a kind of blindness. They stepped back slightly, full of smiles.

They loved the children. When they came they were taken out of Kay's hands. Almost their entire time was spent with them, this bridge which he had helped to erect for them, flowing into the future. He sensed a fresh purpose in their lives.

When, at the flat, he next met Helen, she had drawn back, alarmed.

'What is it?' she said. Perhaps she suspected she was the cause of his sudden affection. It was the first time he has seen her frightened.

'Nothing,' he said. 'I feel fine. Splendid.'

He walked about the room, no longer ashamed.

'Well,' she said. 'You seem very strange.'

'Shall I see you tomorrow?' he'd asked her on leaving.

'If you like,' she'd said, and turned away.

49

Later, when he returned home, he felt this same elation growing, a weight of feeling which the house and its occupants seemed suddenly too frail to withstand. He drew back as he entered, restrained, smiling.

It was a desire to fondle all he possessed that overwhelmed him. He carried the children to bed, embraced them, standing with his arm round Kay as she put out the light.

She had watched him with a half-frown as if his pleasure somehow eluded her. It made her smile.

'Colin's been in such a strange mood, Mother,' she said, as if she might well have confided more to her parent if she had only known how. 'I think it's the prospect of him working on his own,' she added, 'away from the college.'

'Well,' his mother-in-law said, laughing, 'I don't think I disapprove.'

She stood so hopefully on the threshold of their existence, afraid at times, out of her anxiety, to look in.

And really, in that gesture, the closing of her eyes to a conflict – frightened, exhilarated, the whole thing suddenly portentous, larger than life – he saw all that he loved in this other woman: a measure of all those things which he both possessed and had yet transcended. He was moving into new realms, rising beyond her, bearing her along on this new and enormous tide.

Later, at night, lying in bed with Kay and listening to her parents' voices as they, in bed too, talked in the room below, he said, 'Really, only now, you know, am I beginning to get a feeling of things growing.'

'From what?' she said.

'From the past into the future. It's so rare you get such a sense.'

'Isn't it a strain,' she said, 'having my parents here?'

'They always make me feel responsible, more responsible than I feel I really am,' he said. 'And yet now it's as if they're here to confirm, not remind.'

'Yes,' she said.

'Don't you feel a difference?' he said.

'I think so.'

She still bore such heavy wounds about her. It was strange, the way he had forgotten.

'You're glad of so many things these days,' she said. 'It's uncanny.'

'I really feel,' he said, 'that I'm being carried along by things. I don't feel the need to resist. I don't, any longer, feel frightened.'

For a while she was silent. In spite of everything it sounded remote.

'Well,' she said. 'We'll see,' and added, 'My mother's decided to stay a few days longer, after Dad's gone back. She must be feeling pleased.'

And it was Kay's mother he kissed as he left the house the following day; an embrace which, carried from one woman to the other, united all his worlds, bringing together at long last the extremes of his existence.

It was the wholeness he brought to the flat; Helen's surprise was that of someone turning to be greeted by one person – only, at the last moment, to be confronted confusingly by several.

He came to her so full and overflowing. She vanished before him. In the end he was astonished to find that he was not alone.

'I have to go away for a few days,' she told him as she was leaving. 'I won't be able to see you for a while.'

'That's okay,' he said. 'Where are you going?'

'Oh. A conference.' She shrugged.

'With your husband.'

'That's right."

'And you can't get out of it.'

'I go with him every year. It's hardly worth the trouble to make this an exception.'

'What does your husband do?' he said. He had asked her several times before.

'Oh. Nothing important.'

'You find it pretty boring?' he suggested.

'More or less.' She smiled, watching his expression.

'You find most kinds of work boring,' he said. 'I mean, you have much the same response to mine.'

'It's a means to an end,' she said. 'At least, that's what they tell me.'

He laughed, too, at his own intentness and said, 'Well, in any case, I'll miss you.'

'I'll miss you, too,' she said.

Yet once she had gone he felt relieved.

It was a fight; like a frontier he was pushing back. He needed time to consolidate the ground.

When she came back she seemed changed, perhaps more distant. She was slow, even thoughtful.

'What will happen to all this,' he said, 'when your husband finds out?'

'When?'

'Or if.'

'I don't know.' She seemed surprised. 'Why?' she said. 'Do you want to end it?'

'No.'

'Not just yet?'

'Not ever. I can't see any end to it.'

She looked at him in disbelief, with a kind of irritation. Then, as she was leaving, she said, 'You never asked about the conference.'

'I'm sorry,' he said. 'I didn't think you'd want me to.' He had never really believed her excuse for going away.

'It doesn't matter,' she said.

'I'd like to know,' he said.

'Really. It's not important.' She began to laugh.

Curiously, it was his distrust of her that made her real.

There had been one moment, the day before Kay's mother was due to leave, when he and his mother-in-law had been left together in the house and he had been about to tell her everything. He had arranged to go to the flat and before he left he turned to her with the confession on his lips. He had the distinct impression she would have been pleased to hear it. Instead, he stooped forward and kissed her cheek saying, 'I have to go. Look after the children,' as if he were leaving them for good.

She had merely said, 'All right, I will,' looking up at him with a kind of pleasure, impatient, half-amused.

He was happier than he had ever been. And he was never happier now than when he was returning home, or than when he was about to leave home to go to the flat and looked up, thinking of it and her.

The attention he paid Kay never flagged. One evening, after taking her out to dinner and getting drunk, he told her suddenly, in his expansive mood, that he thought he ought to take a room somewhere, away from the house. He was surprised himself that the thing had come out so directly.

'To do what?' she said.

'Really to get down to work, I suppose. I'm not getting through all I want to at the college.'

She looked puzzled. After a moment she said, 'Well, if you really have to.' Then adding, 'Can you afford it?'

'I don't know.' He held her hand, reassuring her. 'I'll have to think about it. It's only a suggestion.'

Yet, now the college was back in session and the area crowded with students, he had to plan his meetings at the flat with greater care.

With this restriction came a sort of restlessness.

'What are we supposed to be doing here?' he asked Helen on one occasion.

'Doing?'

'Is it just something of a convenience to you?'

'If it was,' she said, 'I'd hardly go to all this trouble.'

'But then, by making it difficult you can give it a kind of significance.'

'Why do you think I come here?' she said.

'I don't know,' he said quickly. After a moment he added, 'I suppose I'm too frightened of losing you to answer that.'

On another occasion he said, 'Perhaps we'd better discuss it. What it is, I mean, we're doing here.'

'Discuss!' she said, lighting a cigarette. She flicked the lighter shut and turned away.

He began to feel cheated. To feel, that is, that he was cheating himself. As time passed he wanted to make something out of his feelings for her. Nothing stood still.

Kay had grown quieter, more contained. In return, his own response grew more deliberate. The continual need each time he returned home of having to court her, to reassure himself of her, to question her by his gestures as well as by his silences, began to wear him down.

He began secretly to despise her: someone who could so easily be deceived. Her naïvety irritated him. If she knew something why didn't it come out?

54

He began to hate his work.

He had in any case done very little. It had become quite meaningless and absurd.

At first he had carried on with it, borne along by these new forces that had flooded into his life. Yet quite soon it began to seem like one more appendage to his past, one more impediment, that sense of delay which persisted at every level of his life, frustrating him, holding him back.

It was all wearing very thin.

One evening at the flat he decided he would have to tell Kay what was happening.

Helen was lying on the bed, gazing at the ceiling, smoking. He no longer felt any obligation to avoid either her body or her looks.

'What do you think?' he said when he saw her lack of response.

'You do what you think fit,' she said, gazing at the ceiling. 'In any case, I would have thought she knew by now.'

'I don't think so.'

'Well . . .' She glanced across at him and half-smiled.

'You don't mind if I tell her?'

She shook her head slowly. 'So long as you don't tell her who I am.'

'Doesn't it make any difference to you, her knowing?'

'What can I do? I suppose I've always assumed she did know, one way or another.'

'And assumed she'd made no bother?'

'She's that kind of woman, isn't she?'

'You don't know her. How can you tell?' Absurdly, he found himself in the situation of defending Kay against her.

'No, I don't know,' she said, apparently contented.

'Really, all you're wanting here is a position you can withdraw from,' he told her, 'any time you like.'

'I suppose I do,' she said. 'But the same is true for you.'

'Is it?' he said. 'Well, I'm changing that. At least, as far as I'm concerned. I'll tell her. That there is someone else. And I think I'll come and live here the whole time.'

'And leave her?'

'I've no choice,' he said. 'I can't stand this deception.'

'As long as you understand it puts me under no similar obligation,' she said.

'Don't worry,' he told her.

It was the closest they had come to quarrelling.

He wanted to say a great deal more – she lying on the bed, smoking, uncovered, her legs turned on one side.

'What is it?' she said.

'The whole thing,' he said. 'You've given me nothing.'

She didn't answer.

'Don't you think so? I know nothing about you.'

After a moment she said, 'Do you want to go on with it?'

'Is that the solution? You don't want me to feel a thing about you.'

She didn't answer.

'You disown everything about me that I think is worthwhile.'

He stared brokenly at her. Then, finally, he averted his gaze.

'I'm sorry,' she said. 'You'll have to take me as I am.'

He decided to tell Kay.

He had imagined in any case that a time would come when he would announce boldly what had happened; the weight and reality of his feelings would push everything else aside: an authority which Kay, however she reacted, would have to respect.

Yet, having arrived at this point, he still hesitated. The

thought of her distress, the terror and confusion, held him back. He felt too ashamed to approach her directly.

Instead, he sank – so quickly he was astounded – into that mood of despondency which for some time they had both thought to be a part of their buried past, re-opening those wounds so recently healed, querying his life, the complacency and confinement of his existence, the irony of its securities, its inertia.

Kay was broken in two.

It came so swiftly and so perversely, from underneath, that she had no time to prepare herself. She had no defence.

The blacker his moods grew the higher his hopes soared that she would be driven to telling him what he was afraid to confess to her himself: not so much that he was in love as that their lives had reached such an impasse, had become so irrational, that to separate was their only solution. If she could only recognize this he might never have to tell her about this other woman; her life need not be crushed at all.

Yet she seemed as incapable of coming to such a decision, despite his blackness, as he was of revealing it himself. By refusing to offer an explanation he had hoped to make the inevitability of their situation clearer still and had even, being the cautious man he was, begun to map out a system of disintegration so that, if he had to go into decline, he could do so with the sensation that he was, in some sense at least, its master.

As it was, they were running round in circles. The faster he ran, the closer Kay pursued him. So innocent, so gullible: she seemed unable to realize one word would break the spell.

Eventually he told her that he had actually found a room.

'And what's it for?' she said.

'To sort out our differences.'

'What differences?' she said. 'And do you mean literally live there?'

'What else can we do?' he said. 'The longer I stay here the more it drives me into the ground.'

'One of us must be going mad,' she said. 'Only a few weeks ago you said your life had never had so much meaning.'

'I know.'

She gazed hopelessly at him.

'What is it?' she said.

For a moment he was tempted to tell her. 'I don't know,' he said. 'If I did we wouldn't be like this.'

'You mean to go through with it?'

He thought, then, she must know. He gazed at her quite hopefully.

'It'll give us both a rest,' he said. 'And time to sort things out.'

'Yes,' she told him. 'Though all I feel is that if you leave you won't come back.'

'You haven't much confidence.'

'No,' she said.

He was sickened by the whole thing.

A week later he told her he was leaving. He packed a suitcase and went and didn't give her an address.

He was broken-hearted. He didn't know what he was doing. The more he tried to sort things out the more complicated they became. All that he was really aware of in leaving home was the children's faces: not knowing where he was going, nor for how long, they waved cheerfully at him from the front-room window.

What had happened? Everything he had spent his life preparing had crashed to the ground. Nothing had been solved; nothing cleared up or decided.

And having moved into the flat Helen's attitude to him changed too. Or, rather, it became more plainly what it had been – though he had never cared to acknowledge it – before. Dependent on her for some sort of reassurance he realized how meagre her support really was. They met once, at the most twice a week; he sensed in her a fresh resistance. Her need now was to disassociate herself from any responsibility for what he had done: the rupture of his home, the break-up of his life. If anything her silences, those appalling absences from the room, he recognized as her reproach. He grew increasingly frightened.

'You're not responsible for what I've done,' he told her. 'As long as you keep coming here, like you do, that's all I want.'

'It's all right,' she said. 'I understand.'

She didn't come for a week.

She made excuses when she rang. At the same time she tried to reassure him. Finally, on the evening they had agreed to meet, she rang at the last minute and said she couldn't make it.

'Why ever not?' he said.

'I think my husband's begun to suspect,' she said.

'So what?' he said. 'Does that make a difference?'

'For this evening, I'm afraid it does.'

'When shall I see you?'

He felt, perhaps, she'd been frightened too.

'I'll try and get,' she said, 'tomorrow morning.'

He put the 'phone down.

He returned to the bed where he had been lying; where in fact he spent most of his time alone.

A single reading-lamp illuminated the empty room.

He hated to see the place fully lit.

He'd got nowhere.

Through the window he could see the clouds illuminated by the red glare from the city. Somewhere, beneath them, not far away, were his wife and children, his home: everything which, only a few months ago, had been his world; the last things he would ever have wanted to injure, the last things he could have ever done without.

Five

She came the next morning as she had promised. He scarcely noticed. He began to resent her. She was colder than he had ever known her.

'Would you ever leave your children?' he asked her.

'I don't know,' she said. 'The problem doesn't arise.'

'It's a fine indulgence,' he said, 'to think that one can suffer for it alone.'

She had glanced at him then as she might at a man who talked aloud in the street.

'It must trouble you,' he said. 'It might be my decision but you're benefiting from the situation. From the suffering I've caused.'

'What is it?' she said. 'Are you trying to drive me away?'

He watched her for a moment; then, alarmed, he shook his head.

'No,' he said. 'I'm bound to have moods like this.'

'Yes,' she said, and nodded, 'I understand.'

Yet a gap had opened between them. He felt it as soon as she came in the door, the way in which she allowed him to embrace her. He grew, in response, more threatening as if to outrage her not by his but her own desires. He felt her reaction acutely: the casualness which was as much a part of her as anything he knew; a determination, in effect, not to deny herself the pleasure as well as the security which came from holding herself apart.

61

At times she took a delight in arousing him from a distance, glancing up as if surprised to find him contemplating her, revealing herself with an awareness that humiliated him as if implying that her knowledge, even of his deepest instincts, was greater than his own. Underneath it all, however, lay his complicity, a kind of treachery. It seemed that gradually, with his approval, she was deriding the things on which he most relied.

Perhaps he misjudged her. He scarcely spoke to her. She was like some presence he conjured up. He could no longer distinguish between what were her feelings, her motives, and his own. It was like a dream.

Every few days he went home. The length of his visits was dictated very largely by Kay's mood. There was a kind of ruthlessness in her now which he welcomed, at least to the extent that it kept them apart. On her side was this formality, on his a certain amiability which this kind of self-protection allowed. With it he shut himself off from the children's bewilderment, the unmistakable confusion which enveloped everything they did, creating, on the occasion of each visit, an air of normality amounting almost to indifference, as if this arrangement, his sudden removal, the disruption of their lives, were something inevitable if not natural, something for which they should even feel obliged.

Yet his distress never left him, an extension of those feelings when, much earlier, as babies, he had been overwhelmed by their vulnerability, the precarious tenure they held over their own lives.

He delayed telling Kay about Helen.

For one thing, he felt convinced she already knew. To bring it into the open after all his previous postponements seemed an unnecessary infliction. He even believed he recognized in her some appreciation of his concern.

Only her silences, the stony resistance with which she greeted his visits, disturbed him. Occasionally he would glance up from playing with the children to find her gaze fixed appealingly on him, the same look which, unawares, came over her the moment he began to leave, starting for the door. It dragged at him; he resented her. It was her vulnerability he despised, her lack of pride. Some visits, despite the children, he postponed merely at the thought of that ineffectual look. He wondered that he hadn't seen it before, the incapacity to stand alone.

The problem of telling or not telling her, based as it was on the assumption that she already knew, became an increasing distraction. There was this obvious desire not to hurt her more than he could help; and there was the feeling too that, while the thing was as yet unacknowledged, he still had a foot in either camp. When he was at the flat he was determined to tell Kay everything, and when he was at the house he realized the wisdom of saying nothing at all.

He was stifled. Whatever qualification he placed upon it, his life was full of richness; yet there was no one to appreciate it but himself.

One day he rang Coles and met him in a pub.

There, too, he detected the same aloofness. They talked for a while about his work, and about life at the college now he was no longer there.

'I went to see Kay,' Coles said eventually. 'Last weekend.'

'Kay?'

Coles examined him through his thick lenses. 'You don't mind?'

'No.'

'She seems very upset.'

'I suppose she is.'

'There was the friend there I met before. Marjorie.'

'Ah, yes.'

'And her husband.'

'Newsome.'

'Isn't he an artist of some sort?'

'I believe he is.'

'He seemed a very nice chap.'

'Yes,' he said.

He couldn't conceal his disappointment.

'How are you making out, then?' Coles said at length.

'I'm not sure.'

'You're not looking so bad,' he said. 'You're putting on weight.'

'I suppose I am.'

'I suggested that Kay should come over for the weekend to our place,' he said. 'It would give her and the children a bit of a break.'

'That's probably a good idea,' he said.

They talked only a little longer. He left without mentioning any of the things he'd intended. At the last moment, however, he gave Coles the telephone number of his room.

It took him several days to recover from their meeting. It was this rather than anything else which made him tell Kay about the other woman.

He was astonished, then bewildered by her reaction.

It was as if he'd pushed her off a cliff: the spurt of alarm in her eyes, then the cry echoing through his head.

'But you must have known,' he said.

'How could I?' She sounded as embittered by its effect as he was himself.

'You must have known,' he said. 'What do you think it's all been about?'

'I never thought it was another woman,' she said.

'It wasn't at first.' He hung out his arms at the task of explaining. 'She grew out of the circumstances,' he said. 'She didn't create them.'

'What are you going to do?' she said.

'I don't know.'

'Is she married?'

'Yes.'

'Are you going to marry her?'

'It's hardly a question of that.'

'Has she any children?'

'Yes.'

'Does her husband know?'

'I don't think so.'

She turned away. Really she had known, he supposed, yet had never admitted it to herself. He couldn't see why she refused to face it.

'I don't think it's such a good idea to keep coming here,' she said.

'I think I should. If I vanish completely what will the children think?'

'I don't think I could bear it.'

She had started to cry.

He felt embarrassed.

'I'll come on Sundays,' he said. 'If you like, you could be out.'

He hung around for a while, his irritation increasing.

'What do you think?' he said.

Finally, still crying, she had nodded her head.

As he was leaving he said, 'It's perhaps not a good idea, telling everything to Coles.'

65

'Why?' She glanced up at him.

'It'll get around at college, for one thing. For another, I don't want him intruding.'

She didn't answer.

'Have you told your parents about my leaving?' he said.

She shook her head.

'Nor mine, I suppose?'

'No.'

After a moment he added, 'What will you do if they ring up?'

'I don't know.' She waited, then said, 'I'll have to face that, won't I, when it comes?'

He stood in the doorway, regarding her for a little while. 'You know, it's no good making it worse than it really is,' he said.

At first he thought she hadn't heard.

Then she said, 'How could I make it worse, Colin?'

It seemed like some hideous indulgence, her tears, her fatalistic manner, the odd use she made of his name.

'It's not easy for any of us, that's all,' he said.

He watched her shut the door, uncertain of her expression, and came away from the house feeling not merely irritated but betrayed.

The outside vanished. Only the flat itself had any kind of meaning. Within it he was aware, not of himself, but of a robust, plundering animal, heavy and dispassionate, a composite, bits and pieces of them both. Alone in the room, once Helen had gone, he felt disabled. He welcomed her back each time as if waking from a dream.

Some evenings he sat across the room admiring her imperfections, the slight thickening of her waist, the faint mosaic of bruises which, from child-bearing, flawed her

66

stomach; the slight patina of veins. Then, in the shadows, he saw an older, more familiar figure appear, ageing before him.

She never tried to hide. From the beginning she had taken this pleasure in letting him see her. The more frequently she came the more his confidence grew. It was as if he were celebrating a victory, one perversely allowed him by herself. The whole time he reminded himself of his good fortune.

She was a lady.

He had come to recognize this like a man suddenly confronted, after years of confinement, with the world outside, recognizing there something so immeasurably superior to his recent lot that he immediately endowed it with an immutability, a sense of transcendence, all its own: whatever he had thought of it in the past, that first glance established it for ever as something good and meaningful and never-to-be-lost.

So in her he recognized, beyond his own dilemma, beyond those conflicts that engaged him inside and out, beyond his confusion, an imperturbability and intransigence that both distinguished her from and yet united her with the life around. At first he related it to a common feminine property; to that instinct which had told him from the very beginning that women were superior to men: a superiority which lay in this very intransigence, a permanence of spirit, a kind of contentment, as deep and as imperturbable as their capacity to create life. Theirs was an instinct for what was 'for life', fed from their own flesh and blood, from their own outpouring: with it they loved, with it they bore children, with it they died, locked in a communion of spirit. What came out of their wholeness, this sense of life, was something which men could only compose for themselves by edict, that moral order which they fitted onto life like a suit of armour,

67

hoping to contain from the outside what could only be directed from within. So it seemed to him that women were little less than gods, drawn here to love and be loved, to praise and be praised, the sole illumination of men's struggle to exist.

When he told her this she laughed, looking at him with a dulled amazement.

It was the only time, he thought, that anything he'd said had ever surprised her.

He never mentioned this aspect of his feelings to her again. Instead he felt her moving away from him, appalled, like someone retreating from an accident.

One morning he opened the door of his room to find a man standing there, smoking a cigar, one foot on the top step of the stairs. He was wearing a dark overcoat with a fur collar. On his head was some sort of fur hat. He was slightly bigger than Pasmore himself.

'Hello, sport,' he said. 'You in?'

After a moment's hesitation he opened the door wider. 'Yes,' he said, unsure.

'Not very nice weather,' the man said, glancing at the room.

He began sketchily to tidy it up.

'Oh, don't bother. Not on my account,' the man said. He glanced at the papers on the table. 'Hope I'm not interrupting,' he said. 'I know what it's like when you're concentrating.'

'No. It's all right.' He shook his head. His legs for some reason had begun to tremble.

'Nice place,' the man said, and looked round for somewhere to tip his ash.

He offered him the ashtray on the table.

'When I first started up,' the man said, 'I spent the first three years living in a cellar.' He gazed down at the cigarette ends already collected there.

'I suppose you get used to it,' he said.

'Yes,' he said. 'As a matter of fact you do.' He sank down in one of the two easy chairs. 'I came to see you about my wife,' he added.

'Your wife?'

'That's right.' He glanced round at the room, at the bed, the table, the chairs. 'She come here often, then?' he said.

'Well.' He hesitated, then added, 'I suppose she does.' The man indicated he had finished with his cigar.

He leaned over and passed him the tray.

'Thanks,' the man said and watched him as he replaced the tray on the table. 'How much do you want?' he said.

'To do what?'

'To keep away.'

He gazed down at the man quite bleakly.

'I don't understand,' he said.

'How much cash.' The man seemed irritated by his obtuseness.

'You want to pay me money?'

'That's right.'

'You can't really mean it,' he said.

The man glanced up at him. He had taken off his fur hat. Underneath was a thatch of red hair.

'What have you got to lose?' the man said.

'Lose?' He was still dazed, trembling slightly.

'You can't marry her.'

'Well.' He shook his head.

'She's got two children. She's my wife. We rely on

her. All you're doing is making her unhappy, destroying what family life we possess, breaking something up it's taken years to establish.'

Pasmore gazed at him in amazement.

'Have you told her you're coming here?'

'Sure.' He nodded his head. 'I hired a detective.'

'To follow her?'

He nodded his head as if he found Pasmore incredibly stupid. He seemed disheartened.

'Have you told her about this proposition?'

'Why?'

'Well, she's involved in it, I imagine.'

'She's not involved at all. There's me. There's you. I'm making you an offer.'

'Yes. I can see that,' he said.

'I'm suggesting, in other words, that what you have to gain isn't much when you compare it to the harm you can do.'

'I see.'

The man eased himself in the chair. 'How's your wife?' he said.

'She's well.'

'And the kids?'

'Yes,' he said.

'Fine.' After a moment the man added, 'I won't say her life is easy. But then she knew that before she married me. We lived together for a couple of years in that cellar I mentioned.' He waited to see if he recollected. 'She's a very emancipated woman. You know how it is.' He spread out his hands.

'You must be out of your mind,' Pasmore said, 'coming here like this.'

'You won't take the money?' the man had said.

'I won't.' He tried to laugh.

'Ah, well.' The man got up slowly from the chair.

'You make yourself look very foolish,' he said, his amazement growing all the time.

'Does that worry you?'

'No.'

'That's fine, then.' The man crossed slowly to the door.

'Look,' he said. 'I'm sorry about this.'

The man watched him with a slight frown. 'You're not apologizing?' he said.

'No.'

The man glanced round at the room once more. 'Well, then. I'll see you,' he said.

He went out, closing the door.

For quite a while afterwards, no matter what he did, Pasmore could not prevent himself from trembling. His arms shook, his legs shook, his body shook, as if he had been disturbed far deeper than he knew or could acknowledge.

He was woken late the next morning by a knocking at the door of his room.

When he opened it he found the shopkeeper from below standing on the landing. 'I'm sorry to disturb you,' he said, 'but there are some men downstairs asking for you.'

'What do they want?' he said.

'I think you'd better come down,' he told him.

He pulled on a raincoat over his pyjamas and followed the shopkeeper down the stairs.

The street door was open.

Across the street itself a small crowd of shoppers had collected.

On the pavement, by the door, stood four men in dark suits and tall hats. Lying at their feet was a coffin. It was highly polished, with silver rails running round the top and, on either side and at either end, silver handles. Further down the street, amongst the stalls, was parked a hearse.

'Mr Pasmore?' one of the men said, stepping forward and removing his hat.

'Yes.'

'We were asked to deliver this, sir,' the man had said.

'There must have been some mistake.' He looked from one sombre face to another.

'I'm sorry, sir,' the man had said. 'But this is the address. The information we had was that it was urgent.' He indicated the coffin at his feet. 'It's already been paid for.'

'I'm afraid there's been a mistake,' he said. 'There's no one dead here.' He glanced at the shopkeeper. His face, however, was quite impassive.

'What do you want us to do with it?' the man said.

'Whatever you like,' he said. 'It's not required here.'

'The question of refunding's a little difficult, sir,' the man had said.

'It's no concern of mine,' he said. 'I'm afraid you've been made the victims of a practical joke.'

He returned to his room. He locked the door.

After a while he looked out of the window. The hearse was being driven off. Quite a large crowd had now collected.

In the afternoon several wreaths arrived. They were followed a little later by bunches of flowers. Each bore a little inscription. The flowers he returned to the florists, the wreaths he dropped in the bin. It was soon full to overflowing.

One evening a man stopped him at the corner of the street and asked him for a light.

'I'm sorry,' he said. 'I don't smoke.'

The man asked him his name. 'It's Mr Pasmore, isn't it?' he said.

'That's right.'

'I've a few things here,' the man had added, 'I've been asked to give you.'

'That's nice,' he said, and began to smile.

The next moment he was struck in the face.

His eyes closed to the pain.

Another blow struck him by his ear, some violent sensation shot through his knees, and he found himself lying on the pavement. As he struggled round in the darkness a crescendo of blows struck him from above. He called out, rolled one way and another, and tried to get to his feet.

Finally some object struck the back of his head and for a while he remembered nothing else. He heard someone speaking to him, felt another blow in his back then, vaguely, made out a pair of feet walking away. It seemed hours before he managed to clamber to his feet. He felt sick and one eye was almost closed.

Someone passed him in the street, paused, then walked on, glancing back.

When he reached his room he lay on the bed. He thought he might die. His ribs ached, one shoulder felt as if it had been torn off.

When finally he struggled into the kitchen and stood frowning in the light he saw, in the mirror above the sink, a face he scarcely recognized at all. From a mass of blood and bruises peered out a single eye.

73

She rang him up a few days later. 'Perhaps it's better,' she said, 'we don't meet again.'

'Perhaps it is,' he told her.

'I'm sorry about what happened.'

'Maybe I should have taken the money.'

'You'd never have got it. He was just seeing what you were like.'

'Ah, well,' he said.

'No hard feelings, then?' she asked him.

'No. No hard feelings, I suppose,' he said.

He felt relieved as well as disappointed. He felt a little less confused.

He didn't trouble now with anything.

It was as if, somewhere, a last door had closed.

Six

He was woken by the 'phone ringing and for a moment had the impression he was still listening to Helen's voice.

'I hope you don't mind me ringing,' the woman said. 'I got your number from that friend of yours.'

'Oh,' he said. It was Marjorie Newsome.

'I met him the other weekend at your house,' she said.

'Coles,' he said.

'That's right,' she said.

'Is anything the matter?'

'It's Kay, really,' she said. 'I know it's an intrusion. But since your last visit she's been terribly upset.'

'Oh, well,' he said.

'You haven't been there for a while?'

'I haven't been too well myself.'

'Ah, yes,' she said.

'I thought it better to stay away.'

'Well, I hope you don't mind me ringing,' she said. 'Apart from telling you I didn't quite know what I ought to do.'

'No, that's all right,' he said and, after one or two other enquiries, he replaced the phone.

A few nights later she rang again.

She asked him how he was.

'I'm fine,' he said. 'Progressing.'

'Have you seen Kay?' she said.

75

'No,' he said. 'Things have been a bit difficult. I haven't been able to find the time.'

'I think, you know, if you could manage a few minutes.'

'Yes,' he said. 'I'll try and arrange it.'

'I'm sorry to trouble you like this,' she said. 'I'm just frightened she might do something silly.'

'Like what?' he said.

'Oh, anything,' she said.

For a while he was silent.

'Will you see her?' she said.

'Yes,' he said. 'I'll try.'

The following morning he bought several presents for the children.

However, in the end, he packed them in a parcel and sent them off by post.

He called by the house one morning, several days later.

Perhaps she had seen him coming.

She was wearing a red housecoat. She looked drugged, vanquished. The children, still in pyjamas, caught at his legs as he stood in the door.

'I didn't know you were coming,' she said. She glanced past him, into the street, as if she suspected he were not alone.

'Can I come in?' he said.

'I suppose so.'

'Is it all right?'

She turned down the passage.

He shut the door and with the children hanging on him followed her to the room at the rear.

He began to take off his coat. The children tore at the

sleeves. His arms were dragged behind him. 'Now, steady,' he said. The boy finally sat on the floor, watching him with a dazed expression. 'Look, steady,' he said as the coat was taken from him.

Kay had sat at the table. 'What have you done with your face?' she said.

'I had an accident,' he said. Though the swelling had subsided several of the bruises still remained.

She looked away. She scarcely seemed aware of the children. She leaned her head on her hand. Beside her, strewn across the table, were the remains of the children's breakfast.

'Aren't they going to school?' he said. He tried to avoid the blows that were aimed at him.

'Yes,' she said.

'I'll take them round if you want.'

She looked up at a clock on the mantelpiece.

'There's not much point in them going,' she said. 'It's late.'

'It'll give you a break.'

'Yes.' She nodded her head.

'Come on, now,' he said to the eldest girl. 'I'll get you dressed.'

She frowned. Then her lips had curled.

She broke into a heavy crying.

'What's the matter?' he said.

'I don't want to get dressed,' she said. She still held his hand.

'You'll have to,' he said. 'To go to school.'

'I want you to dress her first.' She indicated her sister.

She too, in anticipation, began to cry. She broke into a frantic wail.

77

It was a long, continuous sound, ending in a scream. She sucked in, the air rasping in her throat, and screamed again.

'I should leave them,' Kay had said. 'It's not the first time they've missed a day.'

Yet he felt determined. He released the eldest girl and began to undress the other. Her head sank to one side; her crying increased. It was a kind of withdrawn grief, bitter and resolute: her head was pressed to her shoulder, her body shuddering between his hands. 'It's not worth it, then,' he told her.

She held him away. She tore herself free and ran across the room.

She threw herself into a corner, burying her head in her arms.

'You'd better leave them,' Kay had said.

She got up and went out of the room.

He heard her, through the crying and screaming, going slowly upstairs.

'Look,' he said to the eldest girl. 'Let me dress you.'

After a moment, frightened, she nodded her head.

He dressed her in silence. She sat down beside him as, finally, he fastened on her shoes. Red-faced, she glanced numbly at her hands clasped in her lap.

The boy had gone out of the room. He began to bang with a heavy object in the hall.

Further away he heard Kay's crying, a kind of broken, child-like moaning, scarcely the sound of a woman at all.

'There's my hair,' the girl had said.

He'd picked up his raincoat and pulled it on. The presents he'd brought the children were still in the pockets.

'Are you going?' the girl said.

He nodded, fastening his coat.

'Are you coming again?' she said.

'I might,' he said.

He went down the hall, stepped over the boy, and went out of the front door. He hesitated outside, then walked away.

He turned back when he reached the corner of the square.

In one of the compartments of the hut in the centre of the square an old man was sitting. He sat with his legs apart, his hands supported on a stick. A dog lay near his feet.

He walked back round the square. When he reached the house he stopped by the van.

A child's bucket chair was clipped to the seat by the driver. In the back, amongst the usual debris, was a folded pram. He leaned on the van, looking over its roof, towards the garden. Several women wheeling prams had appeared at one of the gates. The old man in the hut got up.

He took out his key, went up the steps and opened the door.

The house was silent except for a child's voice at the rear. He closed the door quietly and went down the passage to the room. The children weren't aware of his return. The boy was sitting on the floor eating from a pile of raisins spread out beside him.

The eldest girl lay in a chair, still dressed, sucking her thumb and gazing vacantly towards the window. The youngest girl stood with her legs apart over a pool of water. 'I'm a crocodile,' she said.

The boy stood up, put his foot in the raisins, and fell down. He began to cry, picked himself up and ran to him, his arms spread out.

He lifted him up and set him at the table. He gave him a knife and a piece of bread which he began to cut up into tiny, crumbled pieces.

The youngest girl walked stiff-legged towards him. 'I'm

wet,' she said. But when he attempted to take off her pyjamas she cried out, 'No, no. I want them wet.'

'You'll catch cold,' he said.

'No, no.' Yet, despite her resistance, he began to dress her.

He gave them the presents. They quietened. 'Shall we go to school?' he said.

'I don't want to go to school,' the youngest girl had said.

'We might buy some chocolate, then,' he said.

'Oh,' she said, groaning.

'Can I have some?' the other girl said.

When he'd put on their coats he took the boy upstairs and laid him in his cot. He gave him a bottle.

No sound came from Kay's bedroom.

As he took the girls to the front door, however, she appeared on the stairs. Her face was inflamed, her eyes streaming.

'I'm taking them to school,' he said.

'You don't have to,' she said. 'I'll only have to fetch them back in a couple of hours.'

'I'll take them,' he said. From the door he glanced across at the women and the prams in the centre of the square.

'Are you coming at the weekend?' she said.

'I don't know,' he said.

'I'd like to know.'

'Well, yes,' he said. 'I probably will.'

'On Sunday?'

'Yes, all right,' he said.

Without looking back he closed the door.

He didn't go at the weekend.

He didn't know why. The thought of her sickened him: the distress, the demands.

He went a few days later instead, at much the same time as before, in the morning.

The house was in disorder. It even smelt. One of the children opened the door. When he went in he found Kay still in bed. She was crying. She lay turned away from the door, her figure scarcely discernible beneath the blankets. The children, bored, played in their room. Occasionally they came to the door, glanced in, then wandered back.

'I'm sorry about the weekend,' he said.

She didn't answer.

He went down and got the children ready for school. As before, he put the boy in his cot.

When he left, there was no sound from upstairs. He called out, but there was no answer.

He went out, banging the door.

The school the eldest child attended was only a few streets away. Quite often, when he was teaching, he would drop her off on the way to college, taking the younger girl to the nursery round the corner.

Here, in a prefabricated hut in the grounds of a chapel, two elderly women supervised a group of forty children.

He tried to continue with this habit. These were the only times now that he left the flat. On odd mornings, unannounced, he would drop in at the house and collect the children. Sometimes Kay was in bed, sometimes, distracted, she would be wandering round the house.

'Why are you doing this?' she asked him.

'I'm trying to help out.'

'Why don't you come at the time we arrange?'

'Isn't this more useful?'

She shook her head. She frightened him. At times she scarcely seemed able to stand. It enraged him.

'How is your girl-friend?' she asked him.

'She's very well,' he said.

'I suppose her children are looked after by someone.'

'I suppose they are,' he said.

He felt frustrated. Even in the flat her distress pursued him. He couldn't rest.

One morning, after delivering the youngest girl at the nursery, he bumped into Newsome.

He scarcely knew him but for odd encounters in the street: a tall, slim man with thick, fair hair and a rather disjointed look, a little hapless.

'Good God,' Newsome said. 'See who it is.' And added, 'I'll be with you. Hang on a second.'

He dragged a small child behind him in either hand.

When he reappeared, without the children, he said, 'Come on home. Have a cup of something. We were only talking about you as I left.'

He made some excuse.

'For five minutes,' Newsome said.

They began to walk back in the direction of the square.

'How are things?' he asked him.

'Oh,' Pasmore said. 'Much the same.'

The street where Newsome lived was a cul-de-sac, two terraces of Victorian bay-fronted houses ending in a builder's yard. Beyond, rose the roofs of a factory. Some of the houses had been renovated with white, stuccoed fronts; the majority, however, retained their original façade of brick and painted surrounds, crumbling and in some instances decaying altogether. One house had collapsed; the sky was visible through its windows.

'We needn't stay long,' Newsome said. 'I'll give you a lift. I'm off to work in a couple of seconds.'

He led the way to one of the renovated fronts. They

climbed down a narrow flight of stone steps to the basement of the house. The interior was expensively, even tastefully furnished. At a round table in the centre of the room, reading a book, sat Marjorie.

She was in bare feet.

'Oh,' she said. 'What a surprise.'

'Found him at the school,' Newsome said. 'Delivering his bairn.'

'Could you see to the fire?' she said. 'I can't get a spark.'

Newsome knelt down by a pile of coal in the grate.

Against the walls were stacked piles of paintings. Several were hanging up, some of figures in a room; others, apparently more recent, were abstract, the shapes rather like those a tailor might draw before he cut out a suit.

'Have you seen Kay recently?' Marjorie said.

'I have,' he said. 'Yes.'

'How is she?' she added after a moment.

'Oh,' he said. 'Very much the same.'

'I hope you didn't mind me ringing.'

'No,' he said, and shook his head.

'Bill,' she said. 'Get Colin a cup.'

Newsome got up and retreated to the end of the room.

'Smokeless fuel,' she said, looking at the fire. 'Flameless and heatless as well, if you ask me.'

For a while they talked at the table. At the far end of the room Newsome made coffee on a stove. He brought it on a tray then returned to the fire, poking it, then, underneath the coal, sticking in pieces of candle.

He set them alight.

As Marjorie was speaking a door at the end of the room had slowly opened.

A moment later a man appeared.

He was very fat.

A beard, not yet fully grown, covered his chin. It was black, like his receding hair. His eyes too were dark.

His skin, in contrast, was extremely white, his features enormous. A dressing-gown, beneath which he appeared to be naked, was held together by a piece of string.

'Norman,' Marjorie said. She turned.

The man, however, remained standing in the door. He had a slight cast in one eye and as a result held his head to one side, gazing at Pasmore across the bridge of his nose.

'Colin, this is Norman Fowler,' Marjorie said, and added, 'Would you like some coffee, Norm?'

The man smiled but didn't answer. His teeth were very large and white.

'Bill, get Norm a cup,' Marjorie said and Newsome got up once more from beside the fire.

'The coffee's on the stove, Norm,' he said and turning to Pasmore added, 'Well, I'm off. Do you want a lift?'

He got up from the table. His coffee was still untouched.

'Are you coming in, Norman?' Marjorie said.

The man was still standing in the door.

Then, as they turned towards him, he smiled again and, his head still averted, advanced slowly into the room.

As he walked the string on his dressing-gown came apart.

'You're not popping back to see Kay?' Marjorie said.

'I don't think so,' he said.

'How is Kay?'

It was the fat man who had asked. He had now reached the table in the centre of the room and stood with his hands thrust down into the pockets of his dressing-gown.

'Norman was with me when we met Kay recently,' Marjorie said.

The fat man nodded and smiled.

84

'She's very well,' Pasmore said. He added to Marjorie, 'I'll see you. Thanks for the coffee,' setting down the cup.

'Not at all,' she said. 'Come again.'

'Are you going?' the man had said.

Despite all the signs of their departure·he seemed surprised, as if in effect he had understood nothing of what was going on in the room.

'We're leaving, Norman,' Newsome said. He had pulled on his coat. 'I'm going to work. What are you going to do?'

'Oh, I suppose I'll do some work,' he said. He watched Newsome intently.

'Well, goodbye, then,' Pasmore said and followed Newsome to the door.

'Come to the studio,' Newsome said once they were outside.

'I don't know,' he said. 'I haven't much time.'

'I won't keep you long.'

He led the way to a shooting-brake parked down the street. It too was full of paintings.

They drove along in silence.

The journey scarcely took a minute. They turned several corners and the car pulled up by a deserted house.

Newsome led the way round the side and unlocked a door.

The studio was fashioned from a conservatory attached to the side of the building.

Compared to Newsome's own house, the interior was relatively bare. One or two examples of his more recent, abstract work leant against a wall. On the floor, where presumably he did his painting, lay a large canvas. In the centre was a single speck of red paint, put there perhaps by a brush, or a finger, or perhaps dropped there by accident, it was difficult to tell.

'Not very busy,' Pasmore said.

'No.'

Newsome had taken off his coat. He stood looking down at the large canvas, his hands in his pockets.

'For the past few months I've been on with this,' he said.

Pasmore stared at the single speck. It looked like a drop of blood.

Newsome glanced up at him. 'What do you think of Fowler, then?'

'He looks like Captain Kidd,' he said.

'I suppose he does, really.'

'Is he living with you?'

Newsome nodded. He gazed down once more at the canvas.

'What is he, then?' he said.

'What?'

Newsome looked up.

'What does he do for a living?'

Newsome shrugged. 'All sorts.' After a moment he added, 'He's made me a small fortune, in one way and another. He sells pictures, and the like.'

Pasmore glanced round at the white interior. The sole illumination came from the panes of glass in the roof above his head.

'He's living with us at the present.'

'Ah, yes,' he said.

His look reverted to the empty canvas.

'What have you been up to the last few months?' Newsome said. 'Kay says you have some sort of fellowship.'

'Yes.'

'You're working?'

'Yes.'

'Lucky.'

They were silent for a while.

'What's held you up?' Pasmore said eventually. 'Things at home?'

'At home?' Newsome seemed surprised, even startled. 'Oh, at home,' he said. 'No.' He laughed slightly, still unsure. 'I don't know,' he said. 'To paint anything, I suppose, you need a sense of space that, at one level, you can presume is secure. And yet, these days, what is there that can promise that? All I've got is a single blob of paint: I'm beginning to feel that beyond that it's become more or less impossible to go. Anyone who does, you know, I can only see as the most arrogant sort of ass.'

Pasmore gazed at him quite blankly.

Then, as if aware of his look, Newsome glanced up and added, 'Well, it's not your problem, old man. Nevertheless, it's a bit of a stink. What does one believe in, do you think?'

'I don't know,' he said, flushing.

'I suppose, come to that, I could sell this for a few hundred. Or Norman could. It's one sort of statement,' he said, 'and no doubt as relevant as any other.'

They were silent again. Somewhere below the house a train thundered through the ground.

The room shook slightly.

'You haven't come up, then,' Newsome said, 'with any solution?'

'Solution?'

'Answer.'

He shook his head.

'It's amazing, isn't it,' he said, 'how quickly everything drops to bits.'

He moved down to the end of the studio and returned carrying a small painting.

He propped it against the wall, a domestic interior. A woman, perhaps Marjorie, was seated at a table, feeding a baby from a bowl. Beyond her was strewn the bric-à-brac of a kitchen. The picture was painted in bold, heavy strokes and bright, aggressive colours.

'Only ten years ago,' Newsome said, 'I could do that. It's incredible, isn't it?'

For a moment they gazed at the picture in silence. Then he said, 'Look, I'll have to be going. I'm sorry I can't stay longer.'

'That's all right,' Newsome said. Yet he glanced up, it seemed, in some alarm. 'It was good of you to come in any case. I'll drive you home.'

'It's okay,' he said. 'I can catch a bus at the end of the road.'

'Sure?'

He nodded.

'Come again,' Newsome said. 'Any time.'

He walked home.

When he reached the flat he lay down on the bed.

The end had come, he was sure. He no longer knew which way to turn.

He held his head.

The fact was, he no longer knew where he was. He had nothing. As far as he was concerned he might as well be dead.

Seven

He stopped calling at the house.

He spent nearly all his time on the bed, watching the shadows moving on the ceiling, reflections from the street below.

One morning he received a letter forwarded from his home.

When he rang Kay he said, 'What's the meaning of this? The letter is addressed to you.'

'Nevertheless,' she said, 'it's from your parents. I don't want them coming here, that's all.'

'Have you told them?' he said. For some reason he assumed she had.

'No,' she said. 'They're just coming in the normal course of things. I don't want them here. Not with things as they are.'

'Write and tell them,' he said. 'I mean, that it'll be inconvenient at the moment.'

'No,' she said. 'I don't think I can.'

He thought, then, that she might be crying. He waited.

'You'll have to ask them,' she said, 'not to come.'

'All right,' he said.

'Can I rely on that?' she asked him.

'Yes,' he said.

'Are you going to write to them?'

'Yes,' he said.

For a while they were silent. Then, quite distinctly, he heard her sobs.

'Aren't you coming any more?' she said. 'To see the children.'

'I don't think so. Not at the moment,' he said.

'Perhaps you ought to go and see them,' she said, and added, 'Your parents.'

'What about?'

'To try and reassure them.'

'Will that do any good?' He was surprised at the strength of his feeling.

'I think it would.'

'Well, I'll think about it,' he said.

It was a kind of blackmail.

'I see no point in going,' he said.

'No,' she told him.

Yet, the next day, he took the train.

He wasn't sure of his motives. He felt relieved. He sat and waited.

It was very cold.

The journey took three hours. To break the tedium he went into the restaurant car and ordered a meal. It was the first meal he had had for several days. He drank some wine. He felt happy.

The sky darkened.

It began to snow. Thick, white flakes filtered down.

The train ran out onto a plain of red soil. A broad river and the towers of a power station appeared to the east. The clouds thickened. The snow collected against the windows, settled, then, melting, was driven off.

Trees, like squat spiders, slid out of the wilderness of

waste that began to open up on either side. Rows of factories and chimneys covered the horizon. It was like moving into a cavern. A dark and massive gloom settled round the train.

It slowed. Wedges of black and orange rock enclosed the track. It was like a room. The thick flakes of snow vanished. The train ran into a tunnel.

For a while he sat in the relative darkness. The train stopped, then restarted. After a while it ran out into a broad, undulating valley.

On a steep hill on the opposite side stood the silhouette of a town, a mass of towers and domes, with a single spire set at its summit.

The land opened out beside the train. Low hillocks swept up to wooded slopes and, beyond, to moorland shot with snow.

Deep troughs appeared by the track, lakes of black water reflecting the colliery heaps and headgears beyond. Terraces of diminutive houses were strewn out across the slopes.

The train crossed a still river, sunk down between dyked fields. A pathway of coiling arches carried it between the first buildings of the town, past warehouses and mills, then across an erratic pattern of roofs and roadways and yards until it ran in under the side of the steep hill and stopped.

The air was cold.

Occasional squalls of snow blew from the hills to the west.

On the lower slopes were laid out vast screes of houses, studded here and there with colliery headgears. Banners of black smoke and white steam were strung against the cloud.

He caught a taxi in the station yard.

It drove down through the town and out along a main road leading towards the distant hills. The large stone houses on either side gave way to brick terraces and these, in turn, to the vast mounds of the brick estates.

At the foot of one of the nearer slopes the taxi turned off between the houses. It passed between rows of depleted lime trees. The houses grew denser, the roads more winding.

He pointed the way out to the driver and when the car stopped he sat for a moment in the back looking up at the house, its brick front and its curtained windows scarcely different from any of its neighbours.

He got out and paid off the driver, and only when someone came along the road did he push open the wooden gate and walk up the path at the side.

At the back of the house an unkempt garden stretched between decaying wooden railings to a field of long grass, stooped now and grey with winter. The houses backed onto it on four sides. On a mound of earth in the centre a group of small children were playing with a dog.

A tiny porch was let into the back of the house. He rubbed his feet on the mat, lifted the sneck on the door and, without knocking, went inside.

He entered a small scullery. Opposite the door, and overlooking the road, was a window, beneath it a washer and, in one corner, a sink. A draining-board, a gas stove and a table took up most of the space. A small pantry occupied the corner by the door. No sound came from the house. On the stove a kettle simmered. From the oven came the smell of cooking. Moisture on the window obscured the view of the road outside.

He opened a door on the right, crossed the narrow hall and entered the larger room beyond.

It was dominated by a black stove set in the wall opposite the door. Two windows overlooked the road and a single

92

one the garden at the rear. A three-piece suite took up almost the whole interior; a sideboard with a bow-shaped front and a highly polished table surrounded by four chairs had been fitted into the spaces between. Standing in the rear window like an ornamental pot stood a television set designed in the shape of a perfect cube.

It was very hot. A large coal fire blazed in the range.

He was about to call out, moving back to the stairs in the hall, when a figure rose from the settee in front of the fire, rubbing its eyes, then drawing on a pair of spectacles.

Small, slightly built, in her sixties, with a smooth, well-preserved face, rather square and heavy, the woman said, 'Oh, goodness,' struggling to her feet. 'It's you.'

Only slowly did the surprise then the shock seep into her face.

He kissed her on the cheek.

'Goodness,' she said, gazing at him. 'What are you doing here? We were only coming down to see you at the end of the week.'

'Yes,' he said. He glanced round him at the room, at the furniture, then looked out through the window at the field. 'Is my dad at work?'

'He's on mornings,' his mother said. She began to move about the room, lifting papers and clothes from the various chairs. On the table were set out a knife and fork and a plate of bread and butter. They were laid carefully on a table-cloth which had only been half unfolded. 'He should be home any time now.'

He moved round the furniture, keeping out of her way.

'Have you just come up?' she said.

'Yes.'

'Do you want something to eat?'

'I had something on the train.'

93

He stood over the large fire, staring down at it, his hands clasped loosely in front of him.

'Don't you have an overcoat?' she said.

'Ah, yes,' he said as though he had forgotten.

'Well.' She suddenly paused. She gazed across at him with a shy concern, her face flushing. 'How's the family?'

'They're very well,' he said.

He rubbed his hands together, then took off his coat. He went to the front window and looked out into the street, at the identical fronts of the houses opposite. Nothing stirred. The road was empty.

'Kenneth must be walking now,' she said. 'It's what? Nearly a year since we were last down.' She watched him a moment longer. 'Are you up here to work?' she said.

'Not really,' he said.

'Is anything the matter?'

'Oh,' he said. 'It'll wait.'

She glanced quickly at him, then looked away.

'It's nothing to worry about,' he said, smiling. 'How's Eileen and Wendy?'

They were his sisters. They lived in the town.

'They're all right.' She added, 'You haven't been in touch with them?'

'No,' he said.

'Ah, well,' she said and folded up a cloth in her hand.

He sat down. Photographs of his sisters' weddings and his own stood on the mantelpiece.

'Do you want a cup of tea?' she said.

'Yes,' he said. 'I'll have one.'

She went through to the scullery. He heard her lift the meat from the oven. Then she slid the tin back in and closed the door.

After a while she brought in a teapot and put it down in the hearth, by the fire.

'Are you sure you won't have anything to eat?' she said.

'No,' he said, 'really.'

She went to a cupboard set in the wall by the range and took out two cups and saucers.

She set them on the table, then brought a sugar bowl and a jug of milk from the scullery and set them down too. Only then did she pour the tea.

'Susan will be at school now,' she said.

'Yes.'

'How's she liking it?'

'Very much.'

'And Cynthia. Won't she start next year?'

'Yes,' he said.

His mother gave him the cup and saucer.

'I've put the sugar in,' she said. 'Is that all right?'

'Yes,' he said.

'And stirred it.'

She stood uncertainly by the hearth, her hands clasped together. 'Well, I'll just sit down,' she said.

She sat opposite him, in an easy chair, looking out past his head to the field beyond.

'Is the tea all right?' she said.

'Yes,' he told her.

For a while they were silent, gazing at the fire.

The only sound now was of the gas burning in thin jets from the coal.

Then, in the distance, a car crossed one of the roads of the estate.

'Does Cynthia still have her fits of temper?'

'On and off,' he said. 'It'll be easier when she's started school.'

'Ah, yes.' She nodded.

'I'll go and get a wash,' he said. 'Is that all right?'

'Oh. Yes,' she said. 'Are you staying the night?'

'I'm not sure.' He rubbed his face.

'Well, there's always a bed,' she said. And as he went to the stairs, she added, 'I should use the pink towel, you know. It's clean.'

The stairs ran from the hall directly to the back of the house. A landing doubled back at the top; at the front of the house were two bedrooms, and at the back a tiny room on one side of the stairs and a bathroom on the other.

He shut the bathroom door and stood for a while in the narrow space between the bath and the wall staring at the frosted lower pane of the window. The water, heated from the fire below, was boiling in the cistern.

Finally he ran the hot water into the small basin by the cistern, cooled it, then stood with his hands submerged, staring down. He closed his eyes. Only when the burning had subsided did he move.

He let the water run out then dried his hands. His father's razor stood on a little shelf above the bowl and beside it a small mirror. A crack ran down the middle. Whichever way he moved the two halves of his face refused to come together. He turned round, holding his hands to his cheeks.

From below came the sound of the back door opening. Then of his mother's voice. His father invariably came back from work in silence.

When he raised his head he could look out through the clear upper panes of the window. Beyond the field and the backs of the opposite houses, other roofs rose to an arched skyline. Beyond them, to the left, where the estate dipped down, he could see the wooded slopes of the distant hills, flecked with snow.

When he looked the other way he could see, at the head of the estate, the colliery where his father worked.

He went down.

His father was sitting at the table waiting for his meal.

He was smaller than Pasmore, yet with something of the same width of shoulder. Like his mother, he was in his sixties. His hair, however, had retained its natural colour and, with a fringe, was parted and combed back like a boy's. It gave him an unassuming look.

His eyes now, however, were tired and dark.

'Well, it's grand to see you,' he said, and stood up to shake his hand.

He was in his stockinged feet.

'We were just about ready to come down and see you.'

'You still can,' he said.

'Aye.' His father laughed. 'Well, then,' he said. 'And how's the little lass?'

'She's very well,' he said.

'See you look after her,' he said. 'They don't grow on trees.'

'Ah, well,' his mother said. 'You'd better have your dinner.'

'Aye,' he said, and added, 'I feel too excited now to eat. I'm getting too old for yon, you know.' He gestured out towards the pit. 'Two more years and they'll have to tip me out.'

He sat down at the table.

He was rather like a boy. The mother brought the dinner through from the scullery, laid out on a plate, and stood by him while he cut the meat.

'Have you had something to eat?' he said. 'You can have half of this, you know.'

'I've had something,' he said.

97

'Ah, yes.' He glanced up at him.

'Can I get you another tea?' his mother said.

'No thanks,' he said, and sat down.

His father had eaten a mouthful of food then pushed the plate away.

'Ah, well, I can't eat any of that, Mother,' he said.

'You're not leaving it?' she said.

'I can't eat it, that's all.' He stood up.

'Have you had something at work?'

'No.' He shook his head. 'I just can't eat it. It'll save. I'll have it for my supper.'

'You must have something, though,' she said.

'I'll have some tea,' he said, and coughed. The phlegm rasped in his throat. 'I'm full up to my eye-balls wi' dust,' he said. He sat down by the fire.

His mother brought him a pot of tea. He took it with one hand and felt for his cigarettes, finally setting the pot down in the hearth. 'They can't get the young 'uns to stick it,' he said. 'It's only us old-'uns that keep it going.' He lit his cigarette with a large lighter. It was made out of a block of metal, something he had fashioned at work. A tongue of flame leapt from it. 'I'm ever surprised when I get cut that there's not a pile of dust runs out instead of blood. When we're gone it'll all be machines. Press a button and what it took me half a lifetime to do they'll have done inside a week. Progress. One of my mates was killed last week, wa'nt he, Mother? Down a pit at sixty-two.'

'It won't be long,' he said, 'before it's done away with.'

'Aye,' he said, and swung his arm out. 'It'll all be gone and forgotten. And it won't matter any more.' He leaned forward in the chair, his elbows resting on his knees. 'I must be mad.'

'You could come out of the pit,' he said.

98

'What?'

'I could help to keep you. You could get another job.'

'Why, I've got my pride,' he said. 'I can't go giving in.'

Pasmore looked up at his mother. She was standing across the room by the table, one hand leaning down.

'When you were at school,' he said, 'and I was working, at every bit of coal I dug I used to say to myself that's one bit he won't have to dig. I could have dug that entire pit out by myself. Making sure, you know, of that.'

'You shouldn't put so much into me,' he said. 'I mean that. Just for yourself.'

'Nay,' he said. 'Do you know how high it is where I'm working? Thirteen inches.' He measured out the distance between his hands. 'If it shifts as much as an inch I'm done for. I can feel it, riding on my back. Why, you've got to make it add up to something.'

He waited for him to answer.

Pasmore looked away, at the fire.

He glanced away, then, towards the window. In the field a line of children ran past, shouting.

Odd flakes of snow were swept across the garden.

'Well, then. What is it?' his mother said.

'It'll come as a shock,' he said. 'I don't really know how to tell you. But I'm not living with Kay any more.'

His mother sat sideways to the table.

It was as if she'd known all along.

His father had looked up at him; then, as if reassured, he turned away. He stared at the fire. 'Why, then?' he said after a while. It was as if, ever since he had come into the room, they had been building this defence against him. And now he had trampled straight through.

'I don't know why,' he said. 'There's no reason I can

99

put it down to.' He added, 'I just couldn't bear to go on living with her any more.'

His mother shook her head, her eyes wide, startled. 'She's such a good person, though,' she said.

'I know.'

'I don't know what to say,' she said.

They were silent.

'Have you told her parents?' his father said.

'No. We weren't going to tell you either,' he said. 'Not for a while.'

'I wish to God you never had,' his father said.

He got up. He didn't know where to go. He looked about him.

Then he went to the door and closed it.

His feet sounded on the stairs.

'I needn't have told you, I know,' he said to his mother.

'But people have quarrels,' his mother said.

'I know.'

She had begun to cry. But for the blurring of her eyes her expression didn't change. She sat stiffly, as if frozen to the chair.

'How's poor Kay taken it?' she said.

'Well,' he said. 'You can imagine.'

'She didn't want you to leave?'

'No.'

'Is it another woman?' she said. The demand embarrassed her.

'No,' he said.

'Don't you love the children, then?' she said.

'Yes.'

'But they're yours and Kay's. You made them. You can't run off,' she said.

'I don't own them.'

'But they need you.'

'I know.'

She waited.

'Is there another woman?' she said.

'No,' he said, and shook his head.

She covered her face.

He watched the top of her head, the grey, almost whitish hair.

Then he looked back through the window at the field, at the grey grass and the backs of the houses.

After a while the door opened and his father came back in. His eyes were black, startled.

'Well. It was all for nothing, then,' he said. His body was stiff. He stared down at his mother, then turned rigidly to the fire. 'What a waste.'

'No,' he said. 'I don't think so.'

'No?' His father shook his head. He no longer knew what to do with his feelings. 'A man that leaves his wife and kiddies. Why, an animal wouldn't do that.' Then, after a moment, he said, 'What do you think we are? Everybody has a responsibility to their children. A king or a road-sweeper. Do you think you're any different?'

'No,' he said.

'Don't you think your mother and me haven't had hard times?'

'I know you have.'

'And yet we've come through. We've had to. You can't go smashing it all up.'

'I'm not.'

'Aren't you?' his father said. 'Just look around.' After a moment he added, 'I'll tell you. If it's come to this then there's nothing you haven't ruined.'

He went out, leaving the door open. His feet mounted slowly up the stairs.

His mother stood up. She began to clear the table.

She scarcely seemed to move. When he went into the scullery she was standing at the sink, her hands clutching at the edge.

'Perhaps you can try and explain it,' he said. 'To my father.'

'Explain what? There's nothing to explain.'

'I think there is.'

'You don't know, Colin. You don't know,' she said. 'You don't know what you've done.'

She sobbed over the sink, her head bowed, turned away.

'You owe things to people,' she said. 'You do. You can't go shrugging them off.'

'I'm not doing that,' he said.

'Well, I don't understand it,' she said. 'None of us do. You can't go expecting us to.'

'No.' He moved round the tiny space, looking at the bare walls. Moisture ran down in little streams over the paint. 'It's better that I told you, though,' he said. 'That's all.'

He went through to the room and got his coat.

He'd reached the back door, opening it, before she said, 'Where are you going?'

'I don't know,' he said. 'I might walk over to Eileen's.'

'Are you going to stay tonight?'

'I'll see,' he said. 'There's a train I could get back this evening.'

She looked up at him a moment, but whatever she had intended to say she changed her mind.

'All right,' she said. She turned back to the sink.

'Well, then, I'll see you,' he said and went out, closing the door.

Eight

He walked up through the estate. Once, as he passed a gap between the houses, he looked back and saw the roof of his parents' house huddled amongst the roofs of all the others some distance below. As he walked the wind increased, bringing with it small, hard flakes of snow like hail. He held his coat against him, folding his arms.

Soon he came out at the top of the estate. The rows of houses ended at a road running along the summit of the ridge. On the opposite side were a stone church and a large, one-storeyed brick school. On either side of the church and the school, spreading along the ridge to the north and dipping abruptly and steeply to the south, was a row of semi-detached houses with bow windows and small, arched porchways. Beyond, the broad flank of the hill swept across farmland to a second range of hills, the intervening ground broken up by marshy copses and, further off, by the odd, curving crescents of private houses, standing amongst patches of bare trees. To his right, at the northern apex of the ridge, stood the colliery with its twin headgears and its solitary chimney. A black column of smoke swirled over the roofs of the estate below.

He crossed the road and entered one of the front gardens. A driveway of broken paving stones ran down one side, between it and the next house, and in the garden itself the same sort of stone had been used to make a diamond-shaped footpath. In the central patch of soil stood a bird-bath, and on either side a stone dwarf painted in bright colours, one sitting on a toadstool, the other playing a flute. They stood with their backs to the house, facing the road and, beyond, the first houses of the estate. In the triangular areas of soil which completed the shape of the garden were planted several rose bushes cut down to within a few inches of the ground. Over everything lay a thin coating of soot.

On either side of the door were set small leaded windows of frosted glass. The central pane was tinted red. Through them, after he had rung the bell, a figure could be seen approaching.

A tall, well-built woman of forty opened the door. She had a square, jowled face and dark eyes which immediately lit up when she recognized him standing in the porch.

'Well, what's this?' she said. 'Have we won the pools?'

She put out her arms, calling out and, rather shyly, they embraced.

'Well, what a surprise,' she said. 'We'd have had the flags out if we'd known you were coming.'

'Perhaps, then, it's just as well,' he said.

She laughed and put her arm in his.

'Nay, we'll go in here, love,' she said, shutting the front door and leading him into the room which overlooked the road. 'The back's all in a mess. I've been cleaning out my cupboards.'

The room was occupied by a heavy three-piece suite in brown leather, and a sideboard, set against the back wall. The three chairs faced the empty fireplace which, like the porch outside, was designed as a small archway. It was set out slightly from the wall in a surround of yellow tiles. The mantelpiece above was occupied by a clock with the hands fixed at ten minutes to two and several family photographs which had overflowed from the sideboard. Here the central ornament was a bowl of plaster fruit.

'We could have had a fire lit and everything if we'd have known you were coming,' his sister said. She left the door open as if at any moment they might have to go out, coming to sit on an arm of a chair. 'Well, and what's London like these days?' she said.

'A bit warmer.'

'You can say that again. We've been going to have snow for three weeks, yet it's never shown up. Not properly. It'll get warmer when it does. How's Kay and the family?'

'They're very well.'

'We had a card at Christmas. Since then, not a word.'

'I'd love a cup of tea.'

'Ah, well, you can come in the back,' she said, 'if you promise not to look.' She stood up, a little flushed at the effort. 'Is Kay with you, then?' she said.

'No,' he said. 'I'm probably going back tonight.'

'Ah, well, if we can't be popular we'd better be kind.'

She stood aside and let him into the hallway. It was divided into two, half given over to the stairs and the remaining passage going through to the narrow kitchen and the back door. He turned to his right into the back room.

It formed an exact square, in contrast to the slightly rectangular room at the front. Three easy chairs with wooden arms stood round a blazing coal fire. A dining-room table and chairs and a studio couch occupied most of the remaining space. It was not unlike his parents' house which he'd just left.

He took off his raincoat and sat down close to the fire. The window at the rear looked out onto a ploughed field. A yellow lorry with red lettering was moving slowly across it, trailing a cloud of white dust; drifting towards the house, the dust had settled on the wooden garage and on the greenhouse beyond, and on the recently-dug clods of earth in the garden. A thin film of it lay over the window itself.

His sister had gone into the kitchen and he heard the pop of the gas as she put on the kettle. When she came in she closed the door and began to tidy up several mounds of clothing lying neatly folded on the chairs.

'Well, that's better,' she said.

'It's fine,' he said.

'My dad fetches us up a bag of coal now and again, so we have no trouble keeping warm. And Jack's got a mate at school whose father's a timber merchant. We get lots of old logs to break up and burn.'

'How are the boys?' he said.

'Oh,' she said. 'They're fine. They'll be off to college soon and I won't see them again. How is it, you think, that men have all the brains?'

She crashed down in a chair, brushing back her hair.

'Have you been to Wendy's, then?' she said.

'No,' he said, and shook his head.

'Oh, big changes on up there and no mistake,' she said, then added, 'That'll be the kettle. How do you like it? Strong?'

She continued talking from the kitchen: her husband, her sister, her children. A great deal was inaudible through the wall. He gazed out at the fields and the lorry which was now descending the slope, spraying out its cloud of lime.

'They've been told not to do it while it's blowing,' she said when she came back in, carrying a tray. 'Just look at it on the window. Jack doesn't mind: he digs the garden before they come. We get fertilized for nothing.'

She laughed, handing him his cup.

'Have you seen our mam?' she said.

'I've just come from there,' he said. 'They're upset.'

'Oh,' she said, 'but what's that?'

'Kay and I have broken up,' he said. 'I thought it best to tell them.' He added, 'Well, to tell you as well. It's better than a letter.'

'Yes,' she said. She gazed at him, alarmed. 'Well,' she said, and put her own cup down on the floor. 'Are you sure?'

'Yes,' he said.

She held her hand against her face. 'My mother and dad were coming down to see you.'

'Yes,' he said. 'They were.'

'I don't know,' she said. She stood up. 'I like Kay a lot. This is a bit of a shock.'

She too gazed towards the window.

For the moment the lorry had vanished. The moaning of its engine came from the bottom of the field.

'Is there anything I can do?' she said.

'I don't think so.' He added, 'You could see my mother and dad when I've gone.'

'Oh, I'll do that.' She shrugged. Then she half-laughed. 'It chops right under you, does that. That's given me quite a shock.' She added, 'You better not do that too often.'

'No,' he said.

'I always felt something would happen.'

'Yes?' he said.

'The way my dad sent you out, as his private army.'

He didn't answer.

'But still. He didn't have much else.' She added, 'It seems none of us did, either.'

'I don't know,' he said.

She sat down at the table, turned away.

Though still smiling he saw she was crying.

'You know, I'd have slain ninety-nine out of a hundred girls you brought home. Kay was the only exception I can think of.'

The door at the back of the house slammed and someone came in coughing. Feet were stamped and hands clapped together.

'Here's Jack. I don't know what he can offer. He's about as illuminating as a spark on a wet night.'

Her husband was a tall, slender man with fair hair and blue eyes and thin, bony features. His eyes lit up, nervously, when he recognized Pasmore.

'Why, Colin,' he said. 'This is a surprise.'

He looked around then, rather like a stranger, for a place in which to deposit a pile of books beneath his arm.

'Here, give them to me,' his wife said, getting up from the table. 'If he puts his mind to one thing he can never fix it on anything else. It's a kind of mental short-sightedness.'

'Oh, she's in one of those moods,' he said, smiling and shaking Pasmore's hand. 'Well,' he added, 'how long are you up for?'

'He's just got here, Jack,' his wife said. 'Don't go asking him how soon he's leaving.'

Her husband raised his eyebrows and sat down.

'I've got a free period, that's why I'm back so early,' he said. 'But if you like I'll go back and come in again. I know where I'm not wanted.'

'Colin's come up with some bad news,' his wife said.

'Oh.' He glanced up at her to read her mood.

'He and Kay have split up,' she said.

His look slowly returned to Pasmore.

'Is that right, then?' he said.

'Yes.' He nodded.

'Well, I'm sorry to hear that.' He gazed at Pasmore intently. Then he glanced down at his hands. 'It's permanent?' he said.

'Yes,' he said. 'I think so.'

'And you'll get a divorce?'

'Yes.'

'What about the children?'

'Well.' He shrugged. 'They'll go to Kay.'

'Yes,' he said.

He looked away.

'Don't you think he's being very foolish, Jack?' his sister said.

He didn't reply for a moment. He gazed intently at the fire.

Then, without raising his eyes, he said, 'No, I don't think so.'

'What?'

'It's no good being married against your will.'

'What about the other people?'

'You don't get married for other people.'

'Even children?' She seemed less shocked than frightened.

'If he doesn't love Kay that's the end.'

'God,' she said. 'And they say it's women who are sentimental.'

'I wouldn't say it was sentiment,' he said.

'And that's the principle you believe in?'

'I wouldn't say it's a principle, either. I'm talking about Colin.' He added after a moment, 'As you know, I like Kay a lot.'

'You must be mad,' his wife said. 'Both of you. Would you do the same with me and the children?'

'Why?' he said. She was standing behind him, looking down at his fair hair. He didn't turn round.

'Well, you know why. If you encourage it in one you can encourage it in another.'

'I'm not Colin.'

'And if you grow bored?'

'Colin hasn't grown bored.'

'If it went sour, then!' She had begun to shout.

'It hasn't gone sour,' he said, 'so don't be so bloody stupid.'

She rubbed her face then said, 'Well, I'll get you some tea.'

Yet she seemed in some odd way contented.

Later the two boys came home from school. They were taller than either of their parents and considerably broader. They wore dark, navy-blue caps with red tassels and dark, navy-blue blazers with a red binding round the seams. They greeted Pasmore deferentially, shaking hands then retiring to the door. The room suddenly seemed too small to accommodate its five occupants. His sister, with all her men around her, seemed suddenly larger and more imposing.

A little later he made some excuse and left.

They came out to the porch to see him off.

'Will you be seeing Wendy?' his sister said.

'I think so,' he said.

It was growing dark. From the field at the back of the house came the moaning of the lorry. Lights had sprung up in the valley and along the road. A stream of traffic was moving out from the town.

'I still can't believe it,' she said.

She'd walked out to the gate with him, holding his arm.

She looked up at him as if, even now, he might easily change his mind.

'Well, then,' he said. 'I'd better be off.'

Jack and the boys still stood in the porch.

The two boys stood motionless, like soldiers.

'Well, look after yourself, Colin,' she said.

He kissed her.

She watched him walk off down the road.

After a certain distance he glanced back. She was still standing at the gate, her arms folded against the cold. Beyond her the lighted porch was empty.

He waved and continued down the road.

He caught a bus into the town.

For a while he walked about the streets, gazing in at the shop windows. He had a meal. He sat for some time in a cinema.

When it was quite late he set off to walk back to the estate.

The house was in darkness when he arrived. His mother got up to let him in.

She hadn't been asleep. He could hear his father turning in their bed.

'Did you see Eileen?' she said.

'Yes,' he said.

She watched him take off his coat.

'And Wendy?'

He shook his head. 'I might see her tomorrow.'

'We thought you'd gone back,' she said.

'No,' he said.

'In any case, your bed's ready,' she told him.

He had the small room at the back of the house. There was a hot water bottle in the bed. An electric heater had been left on to take away the damp.

'Is everything all right?' she said, standing in the door.

'Fine,' he said.

'Well, then. I'll say good-night.'

He heard his father's voice as she went back to their bed. He didn't sleep.

In the night he heard his father get up and go to work. There was the sound of his heavy breathing. Then, in the kitchen, he heard him retching.

His mother got up. Their voices whispered in the room below.

Finally he heard the door shut and his father's boots clacked out as he walked off across the estate.

Very slowly they faded. His mother came past his room and went back to bed. For a long time he heard her turning on the mattress.

In the morning there was a kind of blackness in the house. From the bedroom he looked out over the massed roofs of the estate to the thin edge of moorland in the distance. There the snow had settled: it was lightly outlined against the sky.

'Will you be going back today?' his mother said.

'Yes,' he said. 'I think so.'

'Where are you living now?' she said.

'I have a room,' he said. 'I'll leave the address.'

She still watched him. Her eyes were reddened, her cheeks swollen. At any moment, he thought, she might collapse.

'Your father rang Wendy last night,' she said. 'While you were out.'

'Ah, yes,' he said.

'He wanted someone to talk to.'

'I'll go and see her,' he said, 'before I get the train.'

He laid the fire for her and lit it.

He ate the breakfast she'd cooked for him and helped her to wash up.

'Well, then,' he said. 'I'd better be going.'

She came with him to the front door. She scarcely spoke.

'I'll try and drop in before I leave.'

'Yes,' she said and nodded.

'I'm sorry,' he said. 'At what's happened.'

'Yes.' She stood in the door, her hands clasped together.

'Well, then,' he said, and stepped into the road.

She watched him out of sight.

He caught a bus to the outskirts of the town. At the terminus, the summit of yet another estate, he got out and walked.

The road led up the flank of the valley, away from the town, towards the hills and the moorland to the west. The fields on this side were given over to pasture. Beyond the low hedges an occasional stone farmhouse appeared then, as he climbed higher, several brick houses, large and invariably surrounded by trees. Long driveways coiled away from the road.

His sister's house lay up a narrow, unmade lane. It occupied a terraced clearing in a belt of woodland at the edge of the valley. A drive of black tarmac, inset with parallel lines of white pebbles, led, beyond a pair of wrought-iron gates, to the house itself, a vast, mock-Elizabethan structure with tall chimneys reaching well above the level of the trees.

A stone terrace isolated the house from the garden which, in a series of broad arcs composed of lawns and bare flower beds, ran down to the road on one side and to the cleared edge of woodland on the other.

113

The building was half-timbered. A great deal of ivy had been trained up the lower, brick walls – terminating abruptly where the dark woodwork and the pale yellow plasterwork began.

The front door, a rivet-studded panel, had opened as he came up the drive and a moment later a young woman in a red dress appeared.

She was perhaps in her late twenties, small and rather delicate. She waited until he'd reached her before she offered any greeting. Then, smiling, they shook hands.

'You see,' she said. 'I could have fetched you.' He had 'phoned her from the town. 'It's further than you think.'

'It's all the same,' he said. 'I enjoyed the walk.' And as if he were the host and she the visitor he led the way inside.

They went through to the rear where a large sitting-room, furnished with mock-tudor tables and chairs and a heavy, chintz-covered suite, looked out onto the garden and, beyond, the valley itself.

A girl brought them in some coffee.

'How are they at home?' she said.

'Oh,' he said. 'Surviving.'

'I can imagine,' she said.

He had gone to stand at the window. The city stood out now in a simple silhouette on the opposite skyline. To the west the steep slopes of the estate round his parents' house blended into the final ridge which separated this valley from the parallel one to the north. It was possible to pick out his parents' house. That whole flank of the valley, however, was dissolving in a yellow shaft of light.

'You'll stay to lunch,' she said. 'I've rung Arnold and he's coming specially. He can run you back to town.'

She'd sat down across the room, her legs tucked up beneath her.

'It's very strange,' he said. 'I was thinking, on the way up, looking back at the town: all those houses occupied by women.' He glanced back at her. 'It's extraordinary. The whole thing divided into two.'

'Yes.' She had begun to smile.

'The men go off to war: the women sweep up the house.'

'Some do,' she said.

'Well.' He looked back at the valley. A line of rooks had risen from the trees.

'Some houses are empty,' she said.

'What?'

'Some women go to work. They aren't all like me.'

'Yes,' he said. 'I was forgetting.'

He turned back from the window and sat down.

'I'm sorry about your news,' she said.

'Yes.' He added, 'What did my father say when he rang up?'

'Nothing really. He started crying.'

'Yes,' he said and feeling her eyes on him looked away.

'You've left Kay for good?'

'I think so.'

'You're not sure.'

'Yes. I am,' he said and glanced up at her directly. She was watching him with a slight frown.

'You're an awful ass,' she said.

'Oh, well,' he said, 'it comes to us all.'

For a while they were silent. The girl came into the room, replaced the coffee-pot, and went out.

'What have you come up here to do, Colin?' she said. 'Put the skids under all of us? Aren't we to have any rest at all?'

'I don't know why I came. Partly circumstance.'

'My dad could have done without it for a start.'

'Yes,' he said.

The vast landscape below was beginning to darken. The light flowed out of the clouds in odd, moving patches. It lit up a clump of buildings, some sort of gully, a wood, then slowly drained away.

'What did Eileen think?' she said.

'Eileen? She's a creature of instinct, Wendy, and good intentions. That's really where the rot begins.'

'Not until we come out of test-tubes will we be safe.'

'At least, one can never feel possessed by a test-tube.'

'Well,' she said, looking up, 'do you feel possessed?' And added, 'I wouldn't be too sure.'

A storm had broken by the time Arnold arrived. He came into the room blinking, wiping the snow from his hair. 'Golly,' he said. 'Another few minutes and I might have missed it.'

He was a squat, athletic-looking man with sandy hair and a small, square sandy moustache. His skin was fair and slightly freckled. He wore a dark suit with a handkerchief poking from the top pocket. To some extent, perhaps because of his formality, he looked not unlike one of Eileen's sons. 'Well,' he said, shaking his hand, 'how are you?' turning away before he could answer.

'We're lucky to have Arnold here at all,' his sister said. 'He's been recently moved up.'

'Ah, yes,' he said as if this had escaped him. 'It never rains but it pours.' He took the drink which, at the sound of his arrival, Wendy had poured, sipped it, smacked his lips, said, 'Lovely, sweetie,' kissed her cheek and, putting his free arm around her, added to Pasmore, avoiding his direction entirely, 'What's she been up to, then? Belly-aching about her marital status?'

'No,' he said. 'Mostly mine.'

'She told you that she's up for the council?' he said as if he hadn't heard this reply.

'No,' he said.

'She's just received her nomination.' He drew away from her slightly so that he might admire her. 'As a socialist at that. I tell her nothing about my work. The greatest satisfaction I shall have is the thought of that proletarian council taking to its bosom such a treacherous tick as my wife.'

He released her so that she could mix him a second drink.

'The Pasmores,' he added, 'are the most engaging family I've ever met. They're like horses. Put a pair of blinkers on them, set them in any direction you choose and off they go, as hard as blazes. God help anyone who's standing in their path.'

He took the drink, swallowed it neat and enveloped her in his arms again.

His sister gazed out from her husband's embrace with a slow, watchful candour as if to warn him against any criticism of this display.

Over lunch his brother-in-law said, 'Did Wendy tell you we're adopting a couple of youngsters? Seems we're not up to it ourselves. Don't know which one it is. It's not from want of trying.' He exchanged looks with his wife and laughed. 'Bit of a pickle, really. I thought she'd have had enough with me. I need more attention than any child.' He got up once again to kiss her and, having rung for the maid, brought out a box of cigars.

'Imagine,' his sister said, indicating the snow-swept view from the window, 'some poor little bastard struggling into that without realizing it'll end up here.'

'Oh, well,' his brother-in-law said, 'it could be worse.'

The snow had stopped when they went out to the car. The valley was blanketed with snow. The town stood out in symmetrical black blocks the other side.

'There's always room for you here,' his sister said after she'd shaken hands. 'Apart from that I don't really know what to say. I'll write to Kay.'

'Yes,' he said. 'You've been very kind.'

She stepped back from the window and waved as the car slid off through the crisp snow in the drive.

For a while they drove in silence. The road was covered in snow. No other tracks were visible in it.

As the first buildings came into sight he said, 'I wonder, could you drop me off at home rather than the station?'

'Oh, sure,' his brother-in-law had said.

He seemed embarrassed now they were on their own.

As they crossed the river and passed the factory where he worked he said. 'There's a chap on our board called Swanson. You've probably never heard of him?'

'No,' he said.

'A nice bloke. Quite substantial. But inoffensive, nothing much to look at. His wife's very much the same, a home-bird, self-effacing. You know the type. They've three lovely children.' He paused as he turned a corner, shook a fist at a driver he overtook, and added, 'A year ago he gets a Swedish housemaid. You've heard it all before. But look at it this way. The girl's exactly the type he'd never have come into contact with unless he was where he was, a father, married, substantial, a good home. When he was single he couldn't have got within a mile of a girl like this. They wouldn't have had two minutes for him. And now, there he is, with one inside his house. I mean, to my simple mind that's a terrible sort of irony. As it is, I know for a fact he hasn't touched her. But between you, me and the gatepost I also know for a fact that it's driving him out of his mind.'

'Perhaps he should get rid of the girl,' he said assuming that this was the nearest his brother-in-law would get to talking about his situation.

'So what?' he said. 'The damage's been done. The fissure's open. Get rid of her or keep her: he sees now what a complete crack-up the whole business really is.' He glanced at him as frequently as his driving would allow. 'You've got to admit, old man. That really is the sort of irony that can break the most decent sort of chap, I don't care how deep his attachments lie.'

He dropped him off at the end of the estate.

'I won't drive up,' he said. 'It means popping in for a chat and I should have been back half an hour ago.' He put out his hand across the car. 'Well, I'll see you, old boy,' he added. 'Keep in touch.'

He watched him drive off.

When he got back to the house he found his father sitting alone by the fire.

He had evidently just got back from work. His meal lay on the table, uneaten.

'Is my mother out?' he said.

'She's shopping.'

'I dropped in,' he said, 'to say goodbye.'

His father said nothing, gazing at the fire. His feet were bare, reddened by the flames.

'Well, then,' he said. 'I'd better be off. The train leaves in an hour.'

'I thought you'd already gone,' his father said.

He looked up. His face had collapsed. His cheeks were sucked in between his jaws.

'I'll write when I get back,' he said.

His father looked back at the fire.

'I wish to God,' he said, 'you'd never been born. I wish to God you hadn't.'

'Well,' he said and moved back to the door.

His father sat crouched forward, small, staring at the fire.

'Well,' he said. 'I'll go.'

'Don't come again,' his father said. 'Not ever.'

'No,' he said. 'All right.'

He went out and closed the door.

As he went down the road he saw his mother approaching from the other end.

She hadn't seen him. She was walking through the snow.

He turned up an adjoining crescent, stepped in a gate and, shielded by the hedge, watched her pass.

She walked slowly, carrying a bag which dragged down her shoulder, staring at the ground. Her coat, too large, reached almost to her ankles.

He thought, then, that he might have called out. It was like a figure crossing a stage.

Yet he waited by the hedge and only when he judged she had disappeared did he step out. He continued down the road and caught a bus to the station.

PART II

Nine

He scarcely left his room. He was aware of small things. Like someone inside an egg, a scratching and a scraping: the vague sense of activity outside.

Every few days he went down into the street and bought some provisions, tins, packets of food that would keep. Much of it remained uneaten. He never opened the curtains, lying on the bed all day watching the odd fluctuations of light and shade on the ceiling.

He was in difficulties with the landlord. Inadvertently, on leaving, Helen had omitted to pay her share of the rent. He'd had to provide the whole of it out of his own pocket. What with the upkeep of his house and its mortgage, the maintenance of his wife and children, and in the reduced circumstances of his fellowship, he was finding his commitments more than he could bear. Whichever way he turned he could see nothing but debt and ruin.

Immediately on his return he had rung Kay with the intention of telling her about his visit home. The 'phone, however, had been answered by his mother-in-law, not coldly, nor warmly, but in a tone of such utter disenchantment that when Kay finally came on the line he could think of nothing to say. When she had asked him how he had got on he had answered, 'Well, you can probably imagine,' and at her silence had added, 'Pretty badly,' putting down the 'phone with little more having been said.

He rang again two days later and hearing his mother-in-law's voice hung up without speaking.

He didn't call again for several days. Oddly, the thing he wanted most to tell Kay about was his father's reaction, the ghost of which had pursued him all the way to London and into the very room, lurking amongst the shadows of the chairs and the table, an accumulation of fear and terror he found difficult to control. In the evenings, from between the curtains, he would watch the figures collecting in the street below, the scavengers and outcasts, an army of degenerates about to haul him down.

He wanted at these moments, he could scarcely admit it, to go home to Kay and the children, to bury his head amongst them and beg their forgiveness. All he had ever wanted, from the very beginning, was a feeling of wholeness. All he had ever wanted was to try and set things right.

Occasionally, between dozing and groping into the kitchen in search of food, he wrote letters to Kay: wrote them then tore them up, dropping them in the basket along with his thesis and his papers. Why he couldn't bring his thoughts into focus now that his feelings were so clear he had no idea.

In the end he decided he had no alternative but to go and see her. He got up, washed and dressed, and set off for his home.

It was a bright, spring-like morning. From the start he felt his spirits rise.

Behind him, as he climbed the hill from Bloomsbury, he could see the edifice of St Pancras station rising like a castle from the mist, its upper pinnacles and minarets, lit by sunshine, reaching up into a clear sky. From beyond its tower rose a column of white smoke, bending over like a stalk, billowing slightly and trailing off in a thin, swaying pennant. He glanced behind him as he climbed: the freshness, the increasing clarity of the air, the sudden warmth; he couldn't understand why, for so long, he had shut himself away; why, for so long, he had thought himself finished. Things, after all, weren't as bad as he'd imagined.

He had, in arriving early, anticipated seeing the children before they left for school, and partly at the prospect of hearing them running to the door, and partly out of deference to Kay's own need for privacy, he rang the bell rather than used his key.

There was, however, some delay in answering the door. It was Kay herself who opened it. She was wearing a light blue dress he had never seen before.

He stood for a moment on the step looking in before he realized that in effect she was holding the door in such a way as to discourage him from entering. She looked, he thought, younger than he had ever seen her, glancing up at him with a curious, almost naïve frankness, like a girl.

'Are you in?' he said.

'I suppose so.'

She waited.

'Is your mother here?'

She shook her head. 'She went back a few days ago.' She watched him quite calmly. A blue ribbon fastened back her hair.

'I like your dress.'

'Thank you,' she said.

'Did your mother buy it?'

'Yes,' she said.

He was, then, a little at a loss at what to add.

'Am I allowed to come in?' he said.

125

'I'd prefer it if you didn't.'

He nodded. He didn't quite know why.

'Where are the children?' he said.

'At school.'

'It's a bit early,' he said.

'Marjorie took them.'

He gazed in past her. The house looked very clean, and neat.

'Is this your mother's idea?' he said.

'What?'

He gestured at the house. 'Keeping me out.'

She shook her head. 'I'm not keeping you out,' she said.

For a moment he wasn't sure how to answer.

'If you come on Sundays as we arranged there won't be any misunderstanding,' she said.

Yet he stood on the step gazing stubbornly past her. After all, it was his house. Or was it? Primarily, he supposed, it belonged to his father-in-law who had paid the deposit and the building society to whom he owed a substantial part of the balance. Perhaps the front door, a window, a little of the garden at the back were his and his alone.

'I've still got a key,' he said.

'Yes,' she said.

The furniture too was his. He hadn't thought of his problems in these terms before. They took on a very ugly light.

'The other thing I wanted to talk about,' he said, 'was the money.'

'We can talk about it on Sunday.' She stood now with her arms by her side. 'What time are you coming?'

He wasn't sure. 'Whenever it's convenient.'

'About ten, then.'

He glanced past her once more. The door to the main room at the rear was closed.

'Is Marjorie picking up the children at lunch-time?' he said.

'We do it alternate days.'

'I see.'

'It's my turn tomorrow.'

'It sounds a good arrangement.'

'Yes.'

He waited. 'Well, then,' he said. 'I'll come on Sunday.'

'We'll look forward to seeing you,' she said.

He looked up.

''Bye,' she said, and closed the door.

He was, for a moment, tempted to take out his key; perhaps, even, break the door down as a more practical demonstration of his feelings.

He walked slowly away from the house, his incredulity growing, glancing back as he reached the corner of the square as if unsure he had called at the right address. He hadn't, after all, demanded very much.

Yet everything was the same, even – since the day was growing warmer – to the women pushing their prams in the gardens.

When he reached his room he locked the door.

He sat with his back to the closed curtains, staring at the wall. After a while he lit the gas fire, immobilized, gazing at the wall. He had never felt so low.

On the Sunday he arrived at ten, rang the bell and heard the children running down the passage. For a moment they fumbled with the latch then, slowly, despite their excitement, they pulled open the door.

Wide-eyed they looked out at him.

'Hi,' he said and felt for the first time, imperishably, a stranger.

They looked up at him, full of recognition, yet uncertain what he meant to do.

'Can I come in?' he said.

They nodded, stepping back.

He stooped down and kissed them. In their cheeks he felt the same hesitation, a kind of tenseness.

'Shall I show you what I've brought?' he said.

They nodded, waiting to see what this implied.

'Let's go inside,' he said, 'and see what we've got.'

He picked up the boy and set him on his arm.

He gazed sternly away from him, looking round for Kay as he was brought into the room.

She was sitting by the table, wearing a dress with a large white collar. A white ribbon was fastened round her hair. She was making some notes on a piece of paper.

The room itself was spotless, the floor gleaming, not a toy or a piece of furniture out of place. Even the garden at the back, he noticed, had been tidied. Plants had been set in the borders on either side.

He couldn't help but feel reassured.

'The lunch is all ready,' she said, indicating a row of pans on the stove. 'They just need a light. I've written it down.' She laid the note on the table. 'The meat's in the oven. If you want to use the van at all the keys are on the shelf.' She pointed to the mantelpiece.

'Fine,' he said. He set the boy down and took off his coat.

The children sat across the room and watched him.

'Do you want to talk about the money?' she said.

'Well, it's really a question of economy,' he said. 'But there doesn't seem much point in it at the moment.' He indicated the new coat lying over a chair, the pair of new gloves lying on the table, and the new dress itself.

She lifted up a handbag from the floor and took out a notebook, also new.

'I've set down the weekly expenses,' she said, holding it open at a row of figures. 'Here's what it costs.' She turned the pages. 'We've been short ourselves,' she added. 'My father lent us some.'

'I see,' he said, and added, 'Ah, yes.' His smile had vanished.

She laid the notebook down on the table beside him.

'I'll look it through,' he said.

'Was there anything else?'

He wasn't sure.

'I don't think so,' he said.

She picked up her coat. 'Well, I'd better be off,' she said.

He took the coat and held it, lifting the collar as she slid her arms inside.

'It looks very nice,' he said.

'Yes.'

She pulled on her gloves and picked up her handbag.

'Did your mother buy the clothes?' he said.

'Yes,' she said.

The boy suddenly got off his chair and went to her.

'Oh, I'm going out,' she told him.

He began to cry.

'Are you going?' one of the girls had said.

'Oh, I'll be back before you go to bed,' she said.

She went to the door. The children began to hurry after her.

'I'll be back when you've had your tea,' she said.

He heard the front door close, the clip of her high heels on the steps outside; then, on the inside, the children wailed.

He even thought, for a moment, she might come back. Such a call must be audible across the square.

When he went into the hall the three diminutive figures were standing pressed against the door, the eldest stretching up and reaching for the latch, the other two howling, watching her efforts.

He had to carry them back, one by one, to the room. He gave them the chocolate he had brought. They sat fingering it, tearing at the paper, chewing, still weeping, gazing blankly at the floor.

They cried all morning.

It began to rain. He sat in the window watching the pools forming in the garden.

They ate nothing at lunch. He massed the cold food onto plates and left it on the table.

They withdrew to their various chairs. Crying, the boy fell asleep. He held him, briefly, between his attempts to console the other two. He felt too sick to move.

The rain stopped. The pools in the garden began to drain away. The patch of sky discernible between the surrounding houses was low and heavy.

He brought their boots and coats and hats, the boy screaming now at being woken.

Crying, he ushered them to the door, unlocked the van, pushed back the seat for them to climb inside and set off.

He drove them from park to park. At each deserted playground they got out, were encouraged to climb onto swings where, motionless, they were pushed to and fro, their faces white, their eyes red and swollen, gazing sightlessly around.

From the wet swings he led them to the wet slides, to the wet roundabouts and rocking horses, then back to the van.

At each park the same ritual began, pushing and coaxing, a kind of terror running through him at their incapacity to be reassured.

Finally he judged it was time to drive back. The boy, still sobbing, slumped across the spare wheel and fell asleep.

He drove back past the end of Newsome's street. At least, afterwards, he assumed that this had been his intention. He turned down the road that led in that direction when, some distance ahead, he saw two figures he thought he recognized.

Arm in arm, he was almost on top of them before he recognized Kay and stopped, afraid, in this first instance, of being seen.

The man was tall and heavy, laughing as if, perversely, they knew he was there, she leaning against him as they negotiated various puddles along the street, he making some display of this courtesy, taking her waist.

It was only as they vanished round the corner that he recognized the man at all. It was the figure he had last seen, almost naked, entering Newsome's kitchen, fat, swollen, bearded, a cast in one eye, its head enigmatically averted. Fowler.

He turned the van.

He had little recollection of driving back to the square, merely the sensation of arriving outside the house and stepping down to find his legs trembling so violently that for a while he stood leaning on the door.

By the time she came back he'd achieved, he thought, some sort of composure.

She appeared, smiling, in the kitchen door. The children, having begun their tea and suddenly aware of her, got up and ran to her, embracing her and calling out. For several minutes he was forgotten. He felt a fresh sickness whirling inside him, a desire to get down on his knees and, not unlike them, crawl about the floor.

He sat by the table, his hands spread on its surface,

smiling. The children began to cry now, in recrimination, holding her hands, pulling her down into a chair.

'Now, steady,' she said and, laughing, fell down with them. He caught, beneath her coat, a brief impression of her legs. They were splashed with rain. It was appalling. His entire body was in flames.

Solemnly they took it in turns to kiss her face.

'Did you have a good time?' he said.

'Yes.' She laughed, scarcely looking up, drawing her head back to watch then mimic their expressions. 'Oh, now, it can't be that bad,' she said. Slowly she coaxed them back to their tea.

She sat with them. He poured her out a cup.

'There's no need to stay,' she said, suddenly, looking up as if, for the first time, aware of his presence.

'Oh, I'll see them into bed.'

He sat about the room for a while, occasionally glancing at her, finally getting up and wandering out of the room. He went into the front room which, in the past, he had used as his study, climbed up to their bedroom, the bathroom, the children's room, the guest room, examining them minutely for evidence of any presence other than his own.

He helped to get the children dressed and washed for bed. They looked exhausted now, their faces discoloured and swollen, Kay curiously unmoved by their condition, laughing still and disarming their complaints with long, swaying embraces.

When he came down from their bedroom he found her in the room already tidying it up. 'I'll have to rush round a bit,' she said. 'I've got some people coming in.' And at his silence she looked up and added, 'Are you off, then? I hung your coat in the hall.'

'Well,' he said, 'I suppose I'd better.'

'I hope they weren't too much of a trouble.' She had her back to him, gathering up the remnants of the tea.

'They missed you quite a bit,' he said, and added, 'It's quite disturbing, really. All this: it's not doing them much good.'

'They'll have to learn to live with it,' she said. 'You'll be here next Sunday?'

'Yes,' he said.

'They'll soon get used to it.'

'Who's coming round this evening?'

'A few friends.' She glanced across.

He couldn't believe it.

'I'd better be off, then,' he said. 'It wouldn't look too good, finding your husband here.'

'Have you left the van keys?' she said.

He felt in his pockets. 'I must have left them in the van.'

He opened the door.

'I'll get them,' she said. She came out past him. 'It's always dangerous leaving them there.'

She leaned in the van, extracted the keys, then looked round and checked the doors. He watched her, standing on the pavement, his hands in his pockets.

'Well, thanks for taking them out,' she said. 'I'm sure, really, it's done some good.' She nodded to him and went up to the door. ''Bye, then,' she said, closing it and putting out the light.

He walked slowly away, wondering whether he should stay and see who her visitors might be.

He walked round the square. The curtains had been drawn in the front room and the light put on. The lights too were on in their bedroom on the first floor.

He walked slowly back across the square. Rain had begun to fall again.

Putting up his collar he set off, back down the hill, to his room.

Later he rang her.

The 'phone rang some while before it was answered. The sound of music and voices sprang into his ear before he heard Kay repeat the number.

'I wondered if you'd found some papers,' he said. 'I seem to have dropped them somewhere in the house.'

'I haven't seen anything,' she said as if she had been expecting his enquiry. 'I'll have a look round if you like. Are they important?'

'It doesn't matter,' he said. 'They were just a few notes. I could have lost them anywhere. I was just checking.'

'If I do find anything I'll send it on,' she said.

'Thanks,' he said, and added, 'Sounds like a party.'

'Yes.'

'Anyone I know?'

She was silent for a moment. Then she said, 'There's Arthur.'

'Arthur?'

'Coles.'

'Ah, yes.'

'And Bill Newsome.'

'Oh, yes.'

'I don't think you know any of the others.'

He heard the music change on the gramophone: his gramophone. They were his records, too, purchased from his own resources.

'I'm sorry about the papers,' she said. 'I'll have a look round.'

'Thanks,' he said again.

134

'Good-night.'

There was a brief burst of shouting from across the room then the 'phone was put down.

The night passed as slowly as ever in the street outside, the sound of the crowds returning, of the drunks and singers as the pubs closed: the last footsteps of someone trailing home, then the long hours of silence occasionally broken by the passing of a vehicle; then, so much later, the roar of a lorry, the rattle of milk bottles, the odd, hurried steps of the first workers; the faint tremor through the house of the underground; then more vehicles, slower and more frequent, people passing in a constant shuffle. A faint light finally spread behind the curtains.

He didn't eat. It was as if his stomach had withered away, a gigantic absence at his very centre, a terrible numbness and trembling which, despite all he did, refused to go away.

In his mind he followed the sequence of his family's rising, the preparation of the breakfast, Kay standing in a dressing-gown at the stove, the children playing on the floor behind her; the meal itself, normally the pleasantest of the day, the children dressing, setting off for school. Perhaps it was her turn this morning to collect the Newsomes: driving up that narrow cul-de-sac, knocking at the door, Fowler in his dressing-gown, smiling, extending a hand, his eyes fractionally distorted, his teeth protruding. He held his head. He couldn't rid himself of that image: another man, in public, in possession of his wife.

Even the sounds in the street oppressed him, the ringing of the bell, long since mended, the sound of footsteps mounting to the flat above, the one below.

He locked the door. There was nothing he could do.

He sat quivering in his chair.

135

He held his head, trembling and crying. What on earth could any man want with her?

In the evening he caught a bus at the end of the road and was soon in Islington, approaching the square from the opposite direction and positioning himself across from the house by a telephone booth where, though it was empty, he appeared to be waiting to make a call.

It was early evening. The only illuminated part of the house was the pane of glass above the front door. The glow, however, was so faint that he assumed the family was still gathered in the room at the rear, the door of which, presumably, was slightly ajar.

Periodically he walked up and down, moving off down the road, without losing sight of the house. He kept to the shadows in case he encountered any neighbours.

After a while lights went on at the top of the house; the children were being bathed and put to bed.

He waited. At least, with the house under observation, the worst of his imaginings were now eased.

He walked more boldly round the square, passing by the house, looking up at its door and windows, pausing by the van.

The lights in the upper windows suddenly went out. A short while later they were put on again.

He walked up and down, rubbing his arms.

A taxi entered the square.

It drove round the opposite side. He could see the driver leaning forward, peering at the numbers.

It pulled up eventually by the van and blew its horn.

A few moments later the light in the hall went on, then the door was opened.

Kay appeared, dressed in a white coat. At first he didn't recognize her. Then came the gesture of raising her hand towards the taxi.

Behind her appeared a vaster, broader figure he had no difficulty in recognizing at all.

Marjorie too came to the door, watching them both get into the taxi, calling out, then laughing.

He could scarcely believe it. It was like a tableau, mounted viciously, it seemed, for him alone.

He had scarcely time to step behind the booth before the taxi swept past him and turned in the direction of the West End.

After a while he walked round the square again, past the lighted windows and basements, glancing in, recognizing here and there faces, arriving outside his own front door, pausing and, after some delay, passing on.

He returned to the call box, standing beside it, gazing across at the house. Finally he felt in his pockets, went in the box and called up his house.

He heard Marjorie repeat the number then he said, casually, as though he had scarcely time at all, 'Marjorie, could I have a word with Kay? It's Colin.'

'Colin,' she said, digesting this for a moment then adding, 'Kay, I'm afraid, is out.'

'Oh, well,' he said. 'Never mind. Probably best to call tomorrow. How are you?'

'Very well,' she said.

'And Bill?'

'Oh, same as usual. Battling with the world.'

'Where's Kay gone? Pictures?'

'I'm not sure,' she said. 'I think for a meal.'

'Well, that's good,' he said. 'So long as she keeps eating. Who's she gone with?'

'A friend.'

He waited, looking through the panes of the box at the house, the light on in the hall, imagining her stooped there over the 'phone, swaying perhaps in her leather boots, examining their toes.

'I suppose she won't be back till late,' he said.

'I shouldn't think so.'

'It's very good of you to give her a break.'

'Oh, she's looking after our two tomorrow afternoon. It's share and share alike these days.'

'Well, I won't bother you any longer,' he said. He could hear the television, his television, in the background. 'I might drop in on Bill one day this week. Is that okay?'

'I should think so. Give him a ring before, and fix it up.'

'Fine,' he said. 'I will. Good-night.'

He heard the 'phone put down and watched the light go off in the hall and fade in the pane above the door as she went back to the room.

He watched the house a little longer. All round the square were sons and daughters, husbands and wives, settling down, without him, for the night.

When he reached his room he knelt on the floor.

He lay down eventually on the carpet.

Towards morning he fell asleep, woke, the light forming slowly behind the curtains.

He dug down to some deeper oblivion.

It was as if he had vanished: his hands, his arms, his feet, his clothes; it was as if all their familiarity had been subtracted. They belonged to no one: no one he knew or had any memory of at all.

Ten

In the evening he returned to his post at the corner of the square. Since he was now invisible – to everyone, that is, as well as himself – he took no precautions, walking openly up and down, watching the house and the cycle of lights going off and on. No one appeared either at the door or the windows; it was scarcely conceivable, since he had arrived so early, that Fowler was already inside.

He stamped his feet and rubbed his arms. It was surprising how slowly the time passed. He walked down the road from the square and back again. The house was still in darkness, with just the faint glow escaping from the pane above the door.

He walked round the square again.

He watched the house, gazing across at its darkened windows, walking back round the square in the opposite direction, gazing up very carefully at its door, inviting recognition.

Then, feeling sure that it was too late to expect any callers, he set off back towards the bus stop.

Coming down the road towards him, her arm in Fowler's, was Kay. At least, he suffered from this illusion several times before with a rush of blood he realized his mistake.

He was relieved to reach his room, collapsing in a chair, gazing blankly before him, no longer aware of any of his actions. It was as if he were once again a child, unable to give himself any kind of credibility. Lost, he had severed all connections. He felt hardly any grief at all.

On the Sunday, as she was leaving, with her white gloves and – he now saw – her creamish coat, a white ribbon in her hair, ignoring with the same inexplicable good grace the demands and remonstrations of the children, she had glanced up from the door and said, 'Are you all right?'

'Oh, a bit under,' he said.

'Will you be able to manage?'

'I think so.'

'If you can't I can ask Marjorie or one of the other mothers to pop in.'

He looked up at her quite blankly.

He realized even the sight of his home made him feel sick, the walls and floors and ceilings which, once, he had repaired and decorated with such care.

'I see no reason why you should go out,' he said, 'whenever I come.'

'I think it's better,' she said, watching him from the door.

'I'm sure there are plenty of occasions, apart from this, when they have to do without you.'

'It's as much for your sake,' she said, 'as theirs. In any case, I'll have to hurry. I'm late already.'

She glanced up at him again, then added, 'There's no reason, you know, why you shouldn't take them to your flat. They could even stay the night if you liked.'

'There aren't any facilities there for children.'

'Well, I must be going,' she said. 'We'll have to talk about this another time.'

'Kay,' he said.

'Honestly,' she said. 'I'll have to go.' She waved to the children and closed the door behind her.

'Have you brought some chocolate?' they said.

He sat by them without speaking.

Some time later the boy began to cry, the girls sitting down to watch him then, one by one, they too succumbed, gazing numbly at one another.

He felt nothing about them. He sat in the chair, staring at the wall.

They appeared, finally, to forget about him completely, going off into another room, returning occasionally to retrieve a toy, to stare at him a moment: then they vanished once again, their feet crashing on the stairs and in the room above his head.

With the same lack of feeling he prepared their meal, watching them devour it, subsiding once more into a chair so that, when Kay returned, the plates were still on the table along with the piece of meat which he had sawn at and finally hacked in two.

'How are they?' she said, glancing at the plates.

'Much better.'

They had returned upstairs to play and hadn't heard her arrival. A great deal of crashing and shouting came from the room above.

'If you don't want to spend the day with them,' she said, 'you've only got to say.'

He watched her removing her gloves, laying down her bag, taking off her coat, alert, perhaps antagonistic.

'Why not make it the morning, or just the afternoon?' she said.

She glanced round at him, then, receiving no answer, turned her attention to the table. She began to pile together the various plates.

Beneath her coat she wore a light blue dress threaded through with ribbon.

'I'd better get this cleared,' she said. 'I take it they haven't had any tea?'

His body began to vibrate, his arms to tremble.

The next moment, as she turned from the table with a pile of plates, he had got up and stepped forward and knocked them out of her hands.

He seemed more alarmed by the incident than she was.

For quite some time, it seemed to him, he listened to the sound of the plates cascading and shattering about the room.

Overhead there was a sudden silence. Then, from the stairs, came the sound of running feet.

'I think you'd better go,' she said. 'I'll ask Marjorie to be here next week to hand over the children.'

'It's them I'm thinking about,' he said. 'The sort of people they come into contact with through your naïvety.'

'I don't think my concern,' she said, 'is any less than yours.'

The children crashed into the room. They stared down at the crockery scattered across the floor.

He stood trembling in front of her, his fists clenched, shaking. 'I'd prefer you to be here with them,' he said, 'when I come.'

'That's not your decision.'

'I think you'd better be. And I think, too, I'll call round during the week. If I'm maintaining all this I see no reason why I should be left hanging around out there, freezing, in the cold.'

'If you'll tell me the time I'll arrange it,' she said.

'Any time.'

'Then you'll find the door fastened.'

'I've still got a key,' he said.

'The lock's been changed,' she said. 'A little while ago.'

He watched her then in silence.

He couldn't think what to add.

'Is there any legal justification for that?' he said.

'I've no idea. There's a great deal of moral justification, which is probably more important.'

'Who's put you up to this?' he said.

'No one's put me up to anything. You'd be silly to expect anything less.'

He continued to watch her with a curious kind of fascination, reluctant to go, feeling only now, in opposition to her, a slow sense of reality intruding.

'I may find it unethical, in that case,' he said, 'to continue to provide for the upkeep of the place. At least, to the extent that I do at present.'

'Well, all that,' she said, 'I don't propose to go into. Not in front of the children.'

She had turned to them and sent them to collect various brushes and a dust pan, moving them away from the cracked and crumbled plates.

'What are you trying to do, Kay?' he said.

'I don't understand.'

'Your motives.'

She seemed, suddenly, very calm. Behind her the children had begun to sweep up the plates. 'Don't touch it,' she said. 'Just sweep it. You'll cut your fingers.'

'It all sounds,' he said, 'these arrangements, too practical to be true.'

'I've nothing to hide.' She turned away then, taking a brush from the boy. He was looking at his finger. A spot of blood had appeared at the tip.

She began to sweep together the broken pieces.

It was like another person, nothing to do with his wife. She, like himself, had vanished. This new person, somehow, out of the dissolution, had acquired more than either of them had ever had before.

He went into the front room and sat down, facing the window.

Methodically, from the kitchen, came the sound of sweeping.

After a while she appeared at the door. 'I think you'd better go,' she said. 'This sort of thing: I don't think it's necessary for them to see.'

'They see a lot already, it seems.'

'I don't think so.'

'It's hideous.'

'That's for you to judge.'

The children had come in the door behind her.

'I think it's better you go,' she said again.

He got up, looking round.

Wide-eyed, the children parted in the doorway. He got his coat, pulled it on and went to the front door.

'There's no one,' he said, 'wouldn't feel revolted.'

'Well,' she said, 'about that you can't be sure.'

He crashed the door to behind him.

The whole house vibrated.

He waited several days before he rang Newsome. He waited because during that time he could do nothing at all except stare at the wall, appalled that anyone, not least someone who knew him so well, could be so immune to his suffering.

Finally, when he rang Newsome, he found he was out.

'He's at the studio,' Marjorie said. 'Can I give him a message?'

'Would he mind if I went there?' he said.

She thought about it a moment. 'I don't know,' she said. 'I'm not sure.'

'Oh, well,' he said. 'It doesn't matter.'

'I'll ask him to ring you.'

'It's okay,' he said, 'I'll leave it,' and put the 'phone down.

A short while later Newsome rang.

'How are things?' he said. 'I've been meaning to ring you for some time. Ever since our chat about the divisibility of nature.'

'The what?' he said.

'Why don't we have a drink sometime?' he asked him.

'Oh,' he said. 'I don't know.'

'I'll come round one evening. I don't think I've got your address.'

'No,' he said. 'I'll come round to you.'

The thought of anyone in his room reduced him to tears.

'Well, let's make it this evening,' Newsome said. He sounded incredibly cheerful. He waited, then said, 'Is that okay?'

'Yes,' he said. 'All right.'

'I'll look forward to seeing you,' he said. 'Let's say about eight.'

It grew dark.

The room was soon illuminated by the lights which vaguely penetrated the curtains from the street outside.

The 'phone rang, then stopped.

It rang again a little later.

When he answered, Newsome said, 'Will you be able to make it tonight?'

'I don't know,' he said.

'It's a quarter to nine already.'

'I don't feel too good,' he said.

'How about tomorrow night?'

Newsome waited.

'Yes. All right,' he said.

'Let's say seven,' Newsome said. 'Do you think you'll be able to make it?'

'Yes,' he said. 'I'll get there.'

'The studio.'

'Fine,' he said. 'All right.'

He slept throughout the next day. When he woke the stalls were being wheeled away in the street below.

Beneath the lamps the same dark figures had emerged, sifting through the piles of rubbish. From the opposite end came the line of men with the brushes and shovels.

Soon all the rubbish was mounded in the gutters. The crowd lingered round the last remains, following it as it was loaded into the lorries, arguing briefly beneath the lights, opening bags and bits of paper; then, just as silently, they disappeared.

When he went down the street was empty. He followed the water cart to the opposite end, walking behind the jet of water, standing then and watching it turn and work its way back along the opposite pavement.

In the bus he was carried past the stop. He could no longer co-ordinate his movements. Though he could recollect the studio, recall, even, its brightness, the size and bareness of its walls, the shape of its windows, he couldn't in any way relate it to his actions or to the possible destination he had in mind. He sat, gazing numbly from the windows, watching the district pass by.

Only at the unfamiliarity of the buildings did he rouse himself and, getting up, ring the bell. For a while he walked on in the direction the bus was taking, turning quite arbitrarily at a street corner and walking back the way he had come.

Much later he recollected falling on his bed. He heard the door bell ringing, then, a short while later, a knocking on his door.

He heard Newsome's voice, calling.

The door handle was turned slowly. The door yielded, slightly, against the lock.

It was tried more firmly.

After a while Newsome's steps retreated. Then he heard him trying the kitchen door.

He heard the light switched on and Newsome's steps as he moved around.

The floor creaked. For a while it seemed that Newsome waited. There was the scraping of a chair, a long silence, the occasional creaking of the table as he leant against it, perhaps looking out at the lighted windows of the tenement at the rear.

Then the chair was pushed back, the light turned off and, a moment later, a piece of paper was pushed beneath the door.

Newsome's steps retreated down the stairs then, after a pause, continued in the street outside. There was the slamming of a car door then the sound of the engine revving as the car was driven away.

He didn't pick up the note until the following morning. Newsome had written, 'I traced your address through the telephone number and dropped round when you didn't turn up at the studio. I find these days I spend more time waiting there than I do painting. But then, life is nothing if it isn't surprising. Do give us a ring if you feel like it. I wouldn't mind having a chat.'

Shortly after he'd read it the 'phone rang.

It was Newsome. 'I wondered if I might catch you,' he said. 'We seem to have got mixed up a bit last night.'

He didn't answer. The 'phone was silent.

147

'Did you get my note, then?' Newsome said.

'How's Fowler?' he said.

'Fowler?'

Perhaps he was in the room with him, *déshabillé*, a naked paunch protruding over a pair of naked knees.

'I haven't seen Norman for some time,' he said. 'He's not living here now, you know. He's taken a flat.'

'With his disablement pension.'

'What's that?'

Perhaps Newsome had begun to laugh.

'I've always assumed he'd been wounded or something.' He added, 'Not massacred, that is, by circumstance.'

'Well,' Newsome said. 'That I wouldn't know.'

'How's your painting going?' he said. 'Still on with the red dot?'

'Oh,' he said, 'more or less. One or two things I'm getting sorted out.' He added, 'Come round to the studio and I'll show you. I don't know whether you like that sort of thing at all.'

'I don't think so,' he said.

'We can talk about whatever you like.'

'Where's Fowler live?' he said.

'I haven't got his address.'

'I suppose he's divorced,' he said. 'I mean, I'm assuming that from his habit of knocking around with married women.'

'Yes,' he said.

'I suppose she ran off and left him. I mean, in the circumstances, that would be a reasonable assumption. Maybe I should ring her up. After all, her experience might come in useful.'

'I don't know the circumstances,' he said. 'He has two children.'

'Anyway,' he said. 'Why should I care?'

He stood in the middle of the room, holding the telephone to his ear, gazing vacantly before him.

'Are you free today?' Newsome said. 'I'll pop round if you like for a drink.'

'I suppose Marjorie put her up to it. I mean Kay with Fowler. I can just see Marjorie planting the seeds of that particular romance.'

'I don't know,' Newsome said. 'I know he's very much in love.'

'One of those things,' he said, and laughed.

'Last Sunday,' Newsome said, 'we had to go round to see Kay after you left. She was in a pretty terrible condition.'

'Well, yes,' he said. 'I can imagine.'

He laughed again.

'Look, this is a hell of a thing to talk about over the 'phone,' Newsome said. 'Why don't we meet?'

'I don't think there's much point,' he said and, in the middle of Newsome's answer, rang off.

He rang Kay early on the Sunday morning, before she had time either to go out or even get up. Her voice was low, and startled.

'I want to make it plain,' he said. 'You'd better be there when I arrive. I want no handing over of the children by a third person.'

He could imagine her by the 'phone, dazed, perhaps uncertain about the voice, her eyes half-closed, her face pale, bloodless, at rising.

'And the other thing,' he said. 'You'd better stay while I'm there. It gives the children at least some impression of us together.'

149

He was still speaking when she put the 'phone down.

He stood trembling by the 'phone, staring at the wall.

A little later he got dressed and set off for his house.

He ran to the bus stop, sat impatiently by the door while the empty vehicle lumbered up the hill, sprang off and ran along the narrow streets to the square, past Newsome's cul-de-sac, his feet cracking out in the morning air.

The sound itself stirred him: his heavy breathing, the heat rising through his body.

It was Fowler, however, who opened the door.

He was dressed in a dark overcoat and scarf as if he had himself at that moment just arrived. He examined him steadily over the bridge of his nose. Neither of them seemed quite sure what to say.

'Kay wondered if you wouldn't mind calling a little later,' he said. 'When she's had time to get things ready.'

There was about Fowler the same vagueness of manner and expression that he had noticed on their first encounter in Newsome's kitchen, the remote and faintly disturbed air of someone who was continually finding themselves in two places at once; an effect, perhaps fortuitous, reinforced by the slightly dichotomous focusing of his eyes. He appeared to be listening to a voice speaking from a great distance, an almost mystical air about him, as though his thoughts and gestures were influenced by an authority he alone could hear.

He heard himself say, like someone speaking from another room, 'I'd like to come in and talk to Kay myself, if I may,' and heard this particular voice begin to tremble, the words interspersed with odd gasps and groans, the sounds congealing, caught up in a sudden thickening in his throat.

'If you insist on coming in, I can't prevent you,' Fowler said, his head still averted.

'No,' he said. 'You can't.'

Perhaps he had been mistaken about the beard: certainly he was clean-shaven now.

Old scar tissue spread out behind one eye, running back towards his ear.

As he stepped forward Fowler retreated inside the hall. The door to the room at the rear was locked. From behind it came the sound of the children's voices. They stopped, suddenly, when he knocked.

'Let's go in here,' Fowler said, 'and have a talk.'

He felt his hand laid upon his shoulder. He began immediately to tremble. His arms began to shake.

'I've come to see my children,' he said.

'I know,' Fowler said. 'That's what I'd like to talk about.' Then he added, 'I'd better say, straight away, that it was my idea to lock the door.'

'Well, then,' he said. 'You'd better unlock it.'

Yet he had succumbed already to Fowler's grip and found himself to his amazement being led passively into the room at the front.

'I don't mind you seeing Kay,' he said. 'It's you coming here that I resent.'

Fowler waited, thinking about this it seemed for a little while. 'I don't come here often,' he said. Perhaps he was surprised that there was no rejoinder, for he added, 'I think you must realize. You can still cause Kay a great deal of pain.'

A certain distress was evident in Fowler's manner. One of his eyes began to move loosely in his head. 'I don't think you're aware . . .' he said when the door opened and Kay herself appeared.

She had been crying. He felt the relief flow through him at once.

151

'I'll get ready,' she said to Fowler. 'It won't take long.'

A slow look passed between them. 'I don't know,' he said, and took her hand.

'I shouldn't have asked you to come,' she said. 'I'll be all right.'

It was as if Pasmore wasn't there. 'All I'm objecting to,' he said, 'is Fowler coming here. I don't want him near my children.'

'I know,' she said.

'Well, then,' he said. 'At least that's clear.'

'But the fact is,' she said, 'I do.'

She turned on him quite swiftly. He wasn't prepared. It was as if he'd exposed in Fowler something she didn't wish to see.

She seemed to leap across the room towards him. Tears streamed down her face. He had never, in their long intimacy, seen this agony before.

His only impulse now was to console it.

However, from that one look she had already turned; a moment later, glancing at Fowler, she left the room.

'We'll go,' she said quietly. 'I'll just settle the children.'

As Fowler followed her out she added, 'Could you ring for a taxi?'

He was left on his own.

He listened to Fowler on the telephone, breaking off, as he waited for the ringing, to talk to the children through the kitchen door.

He wondered if they knew he had arrived. The next moment he heard them following Kay upstairs, then Fowler's voice was asking for a cab.

He took the children out in the van, provided them with chocolate and a small carton of sweets, and began his devastating round of the playgrounds. As he pushed and drove and carried he wept, the children glancing up at him, curious, then looking away, unsure what this might mean.

The lunch he had to prepare himself, one price at least for his indiscretion. He bought several tins in a delicatessen and heated them in pans; little of it if anything was eaten.

Nevertheless the place was tidied, the children pacified by the time Kay returned, alone.

She said nothing, coming in, taking off her coat. He felt relieved by her distress.

'I'm sorry,' he said, 'about this morning.'

She greeted the children, talking to them, marking off his exclusion in tiny gestures.

'You forget,' he said. 'I've seen Fowler before. At Newsome's. He came in one day, undressed.'

'I know,' she said. 'He told me.'

'I'm sure you can appreciate, then, any apprehension I might feel.'

'He was ill when you saw him. He was recovering from a breakdown.'

'That's what I've been saying all along. He's unstable.' He felt elated.

'If you'd just got yourself someone who looked normal,' he said. 'But Fowler. He looks as if he's backed into a bus.'

She said nothing. She had begun, once again, to talk to the children.

'It's like a couple of cripples,' he said.

'Yes,' she said.

She held the boy on her knee. Her face was white, heavily shadowed.

'You've got to let me go,' she said. 'I've let you go.'

She glanced up at him. 'It's only your vanity that resists.'

'What?' he said.

There was so much he might have added. He thought, 'These are my children, mine. Wherever she goes, whatever she does, she'll never take that from me.'

She had begun to get up, setting down the children. She picked up her coat and gloves to put away.

'My mother's offered to take the children for a while,' she said. 'I'm going away.'

'Oh, yes,' he said.

She went out to hang up her coat, the children following her and, just as dutifully, following her back. It was like a tribe he'd engendered, nomads.

'Does your mother know about Fowler?'

'Yes.' She looked up.

'I wondered.' Yet he didn't think it could be true.

'You'd better go,' she said. 'I'm tired. I want to get their tea and get them to bed.'

'Where are you going?' he said.

Already she had turned away, making preparations for the tea.

'The sea-side's usually nice at this time of the year. That get-away-with-it-all feeling. Though I suppose with Fowler being artistic he'd prefer a continental holiday. The sun and all that sort of rot.'

And when she said nothing, but began laying out things on the table, getting out pots and plates and bread and jars of jam he said, shouting, 'What am I supposed to do? Let you go?'

She seemed quite calm. The simple mechanism of laying the table had taken her, dreamily, far away.

'I'm not stepping aside, that's all,' he said. 'This house is mine.'

154

'In that case,' she said, 'we'd better leave it.'

'Oh,' he said. 'And go where?'

'Marjorie's.'

'Newsome's!'

Her back was arched over the table: she was leaning forward slightly, gazing out through the window.

As if aware of his scrutiny she turned round. He saw she was crying.

'I can't allow you,' she said, 'to go on hurting me like this. If you hound me like this I'll have to go away.'

He nodded, saying nothing.

'All this belligerence,' she said, 'comes out when I'm on my own. When Norman's here all you can do is stand and tremble.'

There was something here that she didn't like, and he, rather than being discouraged, felt reassured.

The 'phone began to ring in the hall.

'I'll get it,' she said but, as if anticipating such a moment, he had moved quickly to the door. He picked the 'phone up and heard Fowler's voice say, 'Hello?'

'I haven't gone yet,' he said, 'you'd better ring back later,' and put the 'phone down.

It began, almost immediately, to ring again.

He watched her answer it. He had once again, as if fulfilling her prediction, begun to tremble.

He went into the room and sat with the children. They had, in the presence of such a conflict, become a single body, identical in response, almost inert, stupefied. They gazed at him in wonder, their eyes glazed, incredulous, perhaps a little deranged.

From the hall came Kay's voice, quiet at first, then weeping. When she came in, however, her eyes were quite dry. She returned to the table and began to cut the bread.

'When we were young,' he said, 'we only had jam to choose from, and that on dry bread, and only on one slice.'

'Are you going?' she said.

'We had one jam tart, on Saturdays. And on Sunday a currant bun.'

He glanced round at the children.

In the end he avoided their looks. He got up, pulled on his coat and without adding anything further left the house.

Once in his room he fell on the floor, crouched there, holding his head, and crying.

He called out, finally, in disbelief.

Eleven

'I challenge you to meet me at dawn stop fishing rods at thirty paces stop I must remind you that I am very effective with this weapon stop and can strip a man to the bone stop I demand satisfaction stop you are ruining my life stop is there no justice in this world stop.'

'Do you want to send this?' the clerk said.

'I don't know,' he said. 'I wondered how much it'd cost.'

'Well,' he said. 'It'll come to quite a bit.'

He began to count the words with the tip of his pencil.

'Cur have you no cognizance of the agonies of mind to which you and your cold heartedness condemn me stop.'

'Leave my wife alone homebreaker.'

'Adulterer beware.'

'As someone interested in the welfare of my wife and children I must ask you Fowler to make your intentions clear stop.'

'Fowler the unhappiness you are causing me and my children is more than it befits me to describe stop.'

'Fowler do you believe in the sanctity of marriage stop.'

'Oh God is there no end to your infamy stop.'

'Do you want to send all these?' the clerk said, looking at the bundle of forms he had made out.

'No,' he said. 'It's really the price I want.'

'You're going to send the cheapest?'

157

'Not really,' he said.

'Well, look,' he said. 'You choose the one you want and I'll send it. There are all these other people in the queue behind.'

In the end, however, he put them in his pocket.

He walked round the West End for a little while. It had begun to grow dark. Occasionally he stopped at a bar, ordered a drink and, sitting down at a table, took out the empty forms from his other pocket and began to fill them in. He could make little progress.

'Fowler foul Fowler you are ruining my wife.'

He screwed them up and replaced them in his pocket.

It was quite late by the time he reached the square.

For an hour or so he stood by the telephone booth then, when he could detect no sign of life in the house at all, he sat down in the gutter, directly opposite his front door.

Periodically he got up and walked up and down the pavement in front of the house. He had arrived too late it seemed to see the children's light go on and off in their room, and too early to see any visitors depart.

'Fowler my house is little more than a hotel stop any invitation to stay the night must not be misconstrued stop the arrangement is purely nominal stop its motives nothing if not commercial stop.'

Two policemen appeared at the corner of the square and as they glanced in his direction he got up from the gutter and crossed slowly to the front door and rang the bell.

There was no answer.

He rang again and heard the steps of the two men pause on the pavement behind him.

He knocked on the door, stepped back, glancing at the windows and heard one of the policemen cross the pavement towards him.

'No one at home, sir?' he said.

'There doesn't seem to be,' he said.

'Would you mind telling me who lives here, sir?'

'Well, I do,' he said. 'That is, I did. My wife lives here. That is, my former wife.'

'Would you mind telling me your name, sir?'

From further along the pavement the second policeman approached, his hands behind his back, his steps ringing out on the pavement.

He suddenly realized it was quite late. No other lights showed from the windows of the square.

'Well,' he said.

'Have you any means of identifying yourself, sir?' the policeman said.

He felt in his pockets, then glanced back at the house. 'There should be someone in,' he said. 'My children are in there as well.'

The second policeman switched on a torch. He flashed it up at the windows.

'Doesn't seem to be anyone at home, sir,' the first policeman said. 'None of the curtains are drawn.'

'No,' he said.

From his pockets he took several of the forms.

'Could I see those?' the policeman said as he began to put them back.

The second policeman flashed his torch onto the pieces of paper. They read them together, the light lowered to the print.

'You're not living here, then, sir?' he said.

'No.' He shook his head. The second policeman so far hadn't spoken. He glanced up at him then back at the paper.

'These messages, sir: they're a sort of code?'

'No.' He felt in his pockets for some other means of identification. It was all in his room, and what wasn't in his room was in his house. He pressed the bell again, then knocked on the door.

'Your name's Fowler, sir?' He indicated the forms.

'No,' he said. 'It's Pasmore.'

'I wonder, sir,' he said, 'if you'd mind coming down to the station then we could clear this thing up?'

'If you ask the neighbours, they'll tell you who I am.'

'I think we can sort it out at the station, sir.'

He shook his head. 'Oh, well,' he said. 'All right.'

'If it's all as you say, sir,' he said, 'then there's nothing to worry about.'

'No,' he said.

They walked in silence through the streets, the policemen on either side. The odd person they encountered turned, pausing, to watch them pass.

At the station the telegrams were placed on the counter before him and, frowning in the light, his name and address and his occupation were taken down.

It was as if he had been expected, or as if this event were a part of his daily routine. No kind of curiosity or interest intruded.

'Would you mind emptying your other pockets, sir?' they said.

'No, I don't mind,' he said.

He laid the various pieces on the counter before him.

A little pile of debris was brought to light; many of the items surprised him: bits of paper, tickets. A bar of chocolate. A sweet. A student's pen.

'I don't think any of this is necessary,' he said.

'It's just a formality, sir,' he said.

They waited.

When it was completed the man added, 'Now, sir, who would you like to come and identify you?'

'Any of the neighbours,' he said, 'as I told the officer here.'

'In the square, sir?'

'Yes.'

'Could you give us a name, sir?'

He thought for a moment, frowning. There was no one's name he could, at that moment, recollect.

'I know them by sight,' he said.

'How long have you lived there, sir?'

He thought of Coles, in Clapham. It seemed a long way for him to come.

In the end, against all his intentions, he gave them the name and address of Newsome.

He was taken to a small room. It was tiled in white to the ceiling. Two chairs and a table were set down at one side. A barred window, high in the wall, looked out into a lighted courtyard. The barking of a dog and the revving of engines came through the wall.

At intervals steps walked past the door. Somewhere, quite close, was a flight of stairs: he could hear people running up and down and occasionally a voice calling. After a while he began to wonder if he had been forgotten.

Then the door opened and Newsome appeared. A policeman came in behind.

'I'm sorry about this,' he said. 'What a mess.'

'Could you come this way, sir?' the policeman said.

His belongings were handed back across the counter. The two younger policemen had vanished.

'I think it might be as well, sir,' they said, 'not to hang around so late at night.'

'Yes,' he said.

Yet they remained curiously unmoved and had already turned away long before he had reached the door.

'What a thing to happen,' Newsome said. His shooting-brake stood in the street outside. 'Did they tell you they had a call?'

'No,' he said.

'Someone reported you loitering in the street.' He took his arm. 'Would you like to come home?' he said. 'I could do with a drink myself.'

'I think I'll go and see Kay,' he said. 'I think I should have a key to my own home.' His grievance slowly burst inside him.

'She's not there,' he said.

'Who?' he said.

'Her mother came down today and took the kids away. Kay and Norman have gone off on their own.'

He said nothing, staring down the lighted street.

A policeman came out of the building behind them, turned up his collar and set off into the night.

'Why not come home,' Newsome said. 'We can put you up easily for the night.'

'It's okay,' he said.

'I think you should.'

'No,' he said. 'It doesn't matter.'

'At least let me give you a lift.'

'I'd prefer to walk.' Then, as he turned, he added, 'Did they say where they were going?'

'No.' He shook his head.

'Well, then,' he said. 'Good-night.'

Newsome watched him as he walked off, in the wrong direction as it happened, yet he carried on until he thought he was out of sight.

He walked back again, past the station. Newsome's car

had gone. He heard the clocks striking. It was nearly dawn when he reached his room.

Nothing made sense any longer. All those little signs by which he kept in touch with things in and around him had vanished. He had begun to lose all sense of time. When he went down to the street it seemed merely one more adjunct of his confusion, blank, without any opposing existence of its own. He no longer recognized the people around him; they became, simply, embodiments of all those disparate feelings and sensations which poured through his mind, sending him one way then another without any sense of direction or purpose. His head was like a mist. There was no end to himself, no one to appeal to, no one to help him, no one he could even recognize. Everything had been consumed; it was as if he had been eaten up.

Yet he walked, sat down, slept as he had done before. In a way nothing had changed. However hard he looked he could see nothing beyond it. There was nothing else at all; everything was fastened up in exactly the same way. Nothing had been changed; looking back it seemed it had always been like this. There was no way back, no way forward. He was, he knew now, extinct.

Some days he didn't eat at all. Other days he made an enormous meal, emptying tins, only to leave the food half-eaten, sometimes scarcely touched, re-heating it next day, eventually clearing it into the dustbins as it turned to mould. The 'phone had been disconnected. His resources, with his diminished appetite, were just sufficient to cover the rent and food. With the weather growing warmer he no longer used the fire. He never put on the electric light. A pile of candles stood by the bedside; the closed curtains during the day filtered down the light.

At night he lay on the bed with his transistor tuned to a police wave-length. It was like water rushing through his head. The only coherent sounds were these disjointed voices, the evidence of some other world outside: the news of fires, a burglary, someone maimed or killed, a man apprehended with nothing on. For hours he lay in the darkness listening to the unemotional voices, the clicking of switches and the faint revving of cars.

During the day he sat at his desk and wrote. He found there was very little now he could complete. 'What would you do if...' 'In the beginning...' 'I wondered...' 'Eventually, he came to the conclusion that...' He took an abstracted pleasure in writing down these phrases, in thinking of them, sucking his pen, in moving on from one to the next, even in repeating them as if something decisive were being plotted.

One day Coles came to see him. The bell rang and peering through the curtains he saw him in the street, looking up directly at the window. He let the curtain fall abruptly. He waited in the darkened room, listening.

The bell rang again. It was hours before he relaxed.

There were periods, too, when he could do nothing but weep. At some point during the day he would sit down, very much as he might do to a job, an imposition, and begin to cry, a low, dolorous sound associated with no particular feeling, his body thrust forward slightly, his arms folded across his knees, the noise drawn up inside his chest.

One morning he opened the street door and found his father waiting on the pavement.

It was almost midday and the street was crowded with shoppers released for their lunch-hour from the surrounding offices.

His father was dressed in a dark, ill-fitting suit, his hair neatly brushed back from his boyish fringe: some embodiment of that nightmare from which the ringing of the bell had dazedly roused him.

Seeing him incapable of speaking he said, quickly, 'Come on in, then,' as if he had been waiting for him some considerable time.

'I came round to see you,' his father said as he followed him up the stairs. 'We're staying at Kay's.'

'Ah, yes,' he said.

His father hesitated at the door of the room.

'No, come on in,' he said feeling suddenly hospitable, even reassured.

The place was in darkness. After a moment's hesitation he put on the light.

Nothing happened. 'I've no coins for the meter,' he said, and laughed.

He began to grin then quite amiably at his father.

'Don't the curtains pull back?' his father said. He had entered the room quite abruptly, walking to the nearest chair and standing by it, his fist clenching its back, his gaze rigidly avoiding the room.

'Well, I keep them closed,' he said, still smiling. 'You never know who they might let in.'

Nevertheless, after a moment, he pulled one back.

'Your mother's staying at Kay's,' he said.

'Alone?' he said.

'What?'

165

'You're staying with her?'

'Yes,' his father said. His face had reddened now. 'We came down to see the kiddies.'

'Ah, yes,' he said as if this were something he had specifically arranged.

'We didn't intend to come here,' his father said and made some attempt to indicate the room. Its disorder, however, couldn't easily be ignored.

'Do you want a cup of tea?' he said.

'No.' He shook his head.

He glanced hurriedly about him, at the crumpled bed, the litter of paper, tins and rubbish. He moved towards him suddenly as if all this had been designed to humiliate him and turn him from his course.

'You're breaking their hearts,' he said.

'Whose?' He had gone to sit on the bed, remote, as if suddenly unaware of his father's presence. He glanced up, nervously, at the opened curtain.

The door of the room was still open.

A moment later he began to tremble, his arms shaking, as if he didn't know what was going on.

'I'm talking about your kiddies,' his father said.

'They're away on holiday.'

'Holiday. They've been back for weeks.' Then he added more quietly, 'I could fair kill you now. And bloody swing for it. I would.'

He could think of nothing to say. Then, as if reminded, he said, 'I don't think you could. They've abolished hanging. At least, for a trial period, I believe.'

His father raised his hand; he seemed to explode.

An enormous weight had crashed against his head. For a moment he could see nothing of the room at all.

'I was just about to go out shopping,' he said as if

nothing whatsoever had occurred. He looked round for the basket and the money he might need.

'Well, then,' he said, smiling again, 'I'd better be going. At this time, you know, it's pretty crowded.'

He looked round, vaguely, trying to locate his father.

When he went to the stairs he heard him descending behind him, breathing heavily down his nose.

'See,' his father said. 'Are you going back home?'

'What?' he said.

'Are you going back to your children?'

He had turned round in the street doorway to look at him, half-surprised.

'Look, I live here alone,' he said. And as if his father had contradicted him added, 'No, I really do. You can keep a watch on the door if you like.'

His father watched him suspiciously, perhaps even frightened.

In the same reasonable tone he went on, 'I shouldn't come here again. I shan't open the door. I should go home if I were you and forget I existed.'

'Yes,' his father said. 'You'd like that.'

'I would,' he said. 'But, naturally, I can't force you.'

His father looked round him, at the street, at the stalls and the people. 'I've given up all my life,' he said, 'so that you can live here.'

'I don't think so,' he said. 'You handed it over. Don't ask me to get it back.'

He saw his father's eyes expand. His look was black. Some wholly inarticulate violence began to erupt from his father's mouth.

He scarcely heard it. What he did hear, far more clearly, was a kind of high-pitched wail, a sound attached vaguely to a variety of words, but more certainly to a hugeness of feeling he had never experienced or even imagined could exist before. He seemed to descend with it, crying, as if, finally, he had lost his grip on everything and he were falling, physically and in his entirety, through the ground.

Twelve

He saw, first of all, a black disc. It was like a hole; but then a hole without dimensions. It was merely an absence of things. He felt himself sliding towards it. It was, on the one hand, like a hole in the top of his head; it was, on the other, like a hole in the ground. It was both within him and without. He felt himself slipping over the edge. He was drawn into it and consumed by the darkness.

His presence was ignited, by flames, by a heatless inferno; he appeared to pass on into some other dimension. It was a pit, yet the sides were indiscernible: it was bottomless, yet there was no movement either up or down. It was merely an absence and somewhere, at its centre, he hung there, in torment.

Some days Coles came to see him. Usually he sat in silence by his bed, gazing at him through his heavy lenses, occasionally taking his glasses off to clean them, holding them against his knees, his eyes white-rimmed, sightless, gazing blindly down.

He seemed curiously at ease in the disordered room, picking up a chair, setting it down by the bed with the beer or the food or the paper he had brought with him. From the street would come the same shouts, the noise of traffic – and the sound he associated most of all now with the room: the shuffling of hundreds of feet.

Sometimes Coles lit a cheroot.

This was a recent habit, prompted perhaps by the unpleasant odours of the room. 'How long have you been smoking them?' he asked him.

'Oh, it's fairly recent,' Coles said, looking at the cheroot in his hand, as if he were still curious about it himself.

'Any more new vices?' he said.

'No.' He shook his head.

'Socialism, the Revolution,' he said one day to Coles, 'has always intimidated me, you know. In the end it seems to be little more than a reassertion, if in profounder terms, of an existing event: that obsessional relationship one has always known to exist between people and the objects they possess.'

The light glinted from Coles's glasses, hiding his expression.

'The only revolution, in the end, conceivable to me,' he said, watching Coles from the pillow, 'is one which breaks down such a partnership. In a sense I suppose it couldn't be called a revolution. It can only be disseminated by word of mouth, by the touch of one person with another. We're in the hands of revolutionary simpletons. The public event.'

He beat the bed in frustration, looking round.

'Millions have died,' he said, 'in order to bring into existence a state as intransigent as that.'

'Why don't you,' Coles said, 'go and see Kay?'

He laughed after a moment.

'What?' he said.

'Why not?' Coles said.

'Arthur,' he said. 'You must be mad.'

Coles shrugged and didn't mention it again. He asked him instead about his father.

There was little Pasmore could recollect.

'I may have been mistaken,' he said, 'but I had the impression when I stood there, screaming, that his look was one of embarrassment rather than anything else. No doubt he imagined that to have been my intention. That is, as opposed to my behaviour being in any way a reflection of my distress.'

Coles had smiled, puffing out a cloud of smoke.

'I can't find it now, but I had a letter recently from my sister telling me he was ill. His ego's suffered a blow which the digging of coal won't, on this occasion, quite distract. I envy him that. It must be a novel experience. Vulcan, you know, split his father's skull in order to liberate his soul.'

'With an axe.'

'Well, we make some progress, Arthur. You'll have to grant me that.'

Invariably he was in bed when Coles arrived. 'Don't you ever get up?' he asked him.

'I'm only in bed, Arthur,' he said, 'because usually at this time I'm sleeping. I can't sleep at nights for some reason. I find I get up and try and work.'

'Perhaps you should leave it for a while,' Coles said, 'and not try and force it.'

He got up and went to the table and began to examine the sheets strewn there beside the typewriter.

'How's it going?' he said.

'Oh,' he said. 'It's not so bad.'

The following weekend, however, he went out and 'phoned Kay.

171

He rang from a call-box in the tube-station at the end of the street and got no reply.

He presumed she was out shopping – it was a Saturday morning – and waited a little while, standing in the mouth of the tube, in the sun, before he called again.

There was still no answer.

He returned to his room and sat on a chair to wait.

He rang the following weekend from the same box. A woman's voice he didn't recognize answered and after asking for Kay the 'phone was put down, abruptly, and he heard faintly the sound of children's voices, anonymous, perhaps not even his own.

Suddenly Kay's voice said in his ear, 'Yes? Who is it?'

'It's me,' he said. 'I wondered if I could come up and see you.'

Perhaps she had thought never to hear his voice again.

'When?' she said.

'Any time,' he said. 'I'll fit in. I don't have to stay long.'

'Well,' she said. 'I don't know.'

'Tomorrow's Sunday,' he said. 'I'll come up like before.'

'We're going out,' she said, 'in the afternoon.'

'Is the morning any good?'

'There'll be someone here in the morning.'

He wondered, then, if Fowler actually lived at the house.

'Was that Marjorie who answered the 'phone?' he said. 'I didn't recognize the voice.'

'No,' she said. 'A neighbour.'

For a moment he was silent. 'Well,' he said, 'it doesn't look as though you're free.' He turned away, covering his face. 'I'd like to come,' he said.

'We'd better make it next week,' she said.

'Yes,' he said. 'All right.' He had, to his dismay, begun to cry. 'Well, next Saturday,' he said.

'Sunday is much easier,' she said.

'Could I come round one evening?'

'I don't think so.'

'Well, then, next Sunday,' he said.

'Have you anywhere you can take them?'

'I haven't anywhere,' he said. He wasn't sure. 'Can't I keep them in the house?'

'I don't know,' she said. She waited, then added, 'Next Sunday, then.'

The 'phone clicked in his ear; he put it down.

Coles came again during the week. He could measure out his sickness now in the regularity of these visits. There had been times in the past when, waiting for Helen, he had felt imprisoned: the gaoler who came with those meagre rations: the whole ritual of outside sounds, of feet ascending, of handles turning, of doors being opened, the long derangement of waiting.

Coles was no gaoler; a provident, bespectacled angel, he came round the door with a glinting, glaring anxiety, ready to smile from the moment he appeared, keen for his pleasure to be recognized and known.

He helped him prepare his meals in the kitchen, sitting across the tiny table, a celebrant of the same victory, or defeat, he wasn't sure.

When he'd gone he felt his loneliness rising. There was a lot he wanted to talk to Coles about, but he didn't know where to begin. He was aware only of the things he couldn't do, of what it was in his life he had never attempted. From Coles he wanted some sort of confirmation of this, of his disabilities: something which Coles refused to give. He didn't believe it. Coles tried to talk about his visit home, saw the agitation it aroused, and left perhaps a little earlier than he had intended.

He wrote Coles a letter the following day and went out and posted it. It was the first coherent message to have emerged from the turmoil of the past few months. He watched it disappear into the mouth of the letter-box with a kind of disbelief, sceptical of its significance.

The next day he wrote to his father and, after some hesitation, posted that too.

He bought several small toys for the children at the weekend, and some flowers which he kept overnight in a vase.

He set off early the following morning, walking to the house, even then arriving so early that he had to walk to and fro across the end of the square, filling in his time. His excitement grew, the feeling that something familiar and specific was about to happen, the antithesis to the weeks of confusion and alarm.

When he finally stood on the doorstep and rang the bell he felt the blood rushing to his ears: the flowers, the little packages he had carefully tied up the night before burned in his hand.

He gazed rigidly at the door.

He heard the children's voices shouting, the sound bursting dully inside as the inner door was opened. Their hands, then, slid against the front door, the bolts were drawn, the lock turned and the door was pulled clumsily back.

They seemed older, stranger, their hair longer, their looks more curious and remote: a composure in their lives which had scarcely anything to do with him at all. They had been carried now some way beyond him.

'Well,' he said. 'How are you?'

Kay had appeared at the end of the passage. He was aware, vaguely, of her silhouette.

He glanced up, briefly, then looked back at the children.

They stood as if waiting to be introduced, their looks uncertain and surprised.

'Can I come in?' he said to them.

He leant down to lift the boy.

He backed away, frowning, then glanced round for Kay.

'Oh, dear,' he said, more to himself. 'They don't know me.'

He didn't try and lift the others. 'I've brought something for you,' he told them, and stepped into the passage.

Kay had turned round and gone back to the kitchen.

As he entered he saw that the furniture had been re-arranged. Outside, the lawn had recently been cut. The borders either side were full of flowers.

'I've brought these,' he said, holding up his own.

'Are they presents?' one of the girls had asked.

Kay looked brown. Some time, recently, she had been in the sun. He couldn't help noticing the colour, an almost sombre look of health.

Her eyes were heavy with suspicion, a kind of shock. The only medium of recognition seemed to be the objects he had brought.

They took the parcels and, their heads bowed, began to tear off the paper. The coloured tissue and the coloured string, the immaculate knots and strips of ribbon, were soon crumpled on the floor.

Kay had taken the flowers, glancing round to look for a vase, then putting them on the table. Their heads lay pressed together, resting on their sides.

'How are you feeling?' he said.

175

'All right.'

'I've been seeing a bit of Arthur,' he said.

'Yes,' she said. 'He told me.'

Unmistakably, then, he saw this to be a place of which he no longer possessed any part. The room, the house, the garden, it had a momentum of its own, self-contained, self-sustaining. All those marks of his own occupation had vanished. On the wall hung one of Newsome's paintings: curved, crisply-edged wedges of bright colour. At the back of the room was another painting, leaning up against the wall. On the mantelpiece stood a small piece of sculpture, dull-green, bronze, abstracted, a shape he couldn't recognize at all.

The whole place now was a kind of abstraction. The familiar and specific event he had looked for no longer existed. It was as if the room had been pushed out into some vaster existence: no longer was the place his home. Its smallness and intimacy had vanished.

'Are you feeling any better?' she said.

It was like some formality which had to be pursued, rigorously, to its conclusion.

'I think so,' he said.

'How long are you staying?' she said.

'I'm not sure. As long as you like.'

'If you're staying for the day,' she said, 'I'd like to go out.'

The children, having examined their presents, had come back to Kay, standing behind her, holding to her dress.

'I don't want to drive you out,' he said.

'It's not that,' she said.

'I'll just stay for an hour or two,' he said.

The boy had gone back and picked up his present, a small car, glanced at it, then put it down.

One of the girls went to the French window, to the steps leading into the garden.

Yet the room refused to release her. She stood there, looking back at them. Only the eldest girl remained by her, looking up at him with her pale eyes.

'You'll go before lunch, then?' she said and, perhaps recognizing his look, added, 'It'll be much easier that way.'

'Yes,' he said. 'All right.' He went to the window and looked out. The younger girl retreated into the room. He wondered, then, if he might break down; present them with something that couldn't be avoided, that couldn't be ignored.

He gazed out at the garden, aware of the silence behind him.

Aware too, he thought, of Kay watching him. When he turned round, however, he saw she was clearing up the paper left from the parcels.

'Shall we go into the garden?' he said to the eldest girl. She shook her head, frowning.

The boy picked up his toy again, sitting on the floor, gazing up at him, his eyes screwed against the light.

'I'd like to come round one evening,' he said, 'and have a talk.'

'Yes,' she said. 'If you like.'

He cheered up slightly.

'I could come round this evening,' he said.

'I'll be out this evening.'

'How about tomorrow?' he said.

'I think later in the week would suit me best.'

The eldest girl had begun to play on the floor, the boy arranging dolls on a chair with his sister. The atmosphere in the room was one of waiting, for an event to begin, or end, he couldn't be sure.

He sat down after a moment. He wondered to what extent

Fowler had taken his place: the pictures, the sculpture, the rearranged chairs and table, the garden, the flowers. Some vaster spirit inhabited the house.

Kay had gone to the cooking-range at the side of the room. She stood by the sink, lifting in pots from the breakfast. He could see the outline of her cheek and brow, the edge of her eyelid as she gazed down.

She waited, her hands poised on the sink.

The two younger children began to quarrel. The eldest girl got up from her chair and joined them, stooping over a tiny canvas pram, her hands pressing in a cover against its sides. She still wore the same expression, aggrieved, her hands fisted.

'If you're going to see the children again,' Kay said, 'in future, we'd better fix a regular time.' She looked up. 'I mean a time when you leave. And decide before you come what you want to do with them.'

'All right,' he said.

She had half-turned, gazing at him.

He was alarmed himself that he should have revealed anything at all.

After a moment it was uncontainable.

He was aware, then, of the children looking up at him; then of Kay still standing by the sink, half-turned.

He saw too, more certainly, any ground he might have gained slipping away.

He got up and went to the door, shutting it behind him.

He felt the same coldness rise about him. He leant against the wall, his head in his hands.

From the kitchen came the voices of the children.

He went, finally, into the front room and sat down. It was like a waiting-room. He sat with his hands between his knees, staring at the floor, searching now for some device that would make this room, any part of it, his own. His whole body was ignited.

A little later the door opened and Kay came in. She didn't close it behind her.

'Are you going?' she said.

'Yes,' he said. 'I think I'd better.'

He fought, then, for some tiny hold, looking up. The children had come into the passage outside.

He shook his head. 'I can't,' he said.

'If you like,' she said, 'I'll ring up Bill and he can drive you back.'

'I can't leave,' he said. He had begun to cling to the furniture as if already he were being torn away.

He was aware, too, of her fear. Some extension of his own, it seemed to peer down from the room about him.

He heard the children come in, their sudden silence; then he heard too his own voice call out. It came from a distance, across a chasm.

The door was shut. The 'phone was picked up.

Almost the next moment it seemed Newsome came into the room. The children had vanished.

'Look, old man, how are you?' Newsome said. He had leaned down, his hand on his shoulder.

'I'll be all right,' he said, yet he felt nothing leave him.

Newsome's face came down to his. 'Let me get you something,' he said. 'Will you have some tea?'

'Yes,' he said. 'All right.' Yet he shook his head. He couldn't move.

'Let's go in the kitchen,' Newsome said.

He felt his hand tap at his shoulder. 'Let's give you a lift up, then,' Newsome said.

He glimpsed Kay's face as he stood up. 'No, I'm all right,' he said.

179

He walked to the door and through into the kitchen. The children had gone.

On the floor were the toys.

Still on the table, unwrapped, were the flowers.

He began to cry.

'Come on,' Newsome said. 'What is it?'

'I don't know,' he said. He shook his head.

He leant on the table, looking at the floor.

'Come on. Let's hear it,' Newsome said.

'I can't,' he said. He added, 'I don't know what to do. I've nowhere to go.'

'Haven't you your room?' Newsome said.

He didn't answer.

'Haven't you the room, then?' Newsome said again.

'Yes,' he said.

He nodded.

'Let me drive you back.'

'I can't,' he said.

'Why? What is it?' Newsome asked him.

'I can't,' he said again and shook his head.

'Let me take you back,' Newsome said. 'I'll stay with you if you like.'

He suddenly looked round, vaguely, unsure where he was.

Kay stood a little distance away, behind.

He moved away from the table and began to wipe his face.

'I'm sorry,' he said.

'Let me drive you back,' Newsome said.

'All right,' he said. He couldn't stop shaking. Odd intimations of the room came back.

He felt it sinking beneath him.

'I just want you to know,' he said, 'that I'm sorry for what I've done.'

'Now, that's all right, old man,' Newsome said, as if

it needn't be mentioned, as if he had been the one to suffer.

He held his face in his hands. 'I can't go back,' he said. 'I don't know what to do.' And as if this wasn't clear even to himself, he added, 'I don't know what I'm going to do.'

Kay said nothing.

Any signal from her and he would have rushed back, into himself.

Otherwise he was like a ghost. He couldn't let the room go. His spirit was wrapped around it. It was the one thing he knew; the one thing, it seemed, that he remembered.

'Where are the children?' he said.

'Marjorie's taken them,' Newsome said. 'They'll be all right.'

'I love them,' he said. 'I never meant them any harm.'

'Come on, old man,' Newsome said. 'Let me drive you back.'

He still held his face. 'I didn't want this to happen.'

He looked up at Kay, afraid of recognizing anything at all.

He was a kind of monster: some hunger that had driven them back. He couldn't imagine how it had ever begun.

Yet Kay, all he saw, was something spun out from his own hysteria, intangible, far off.

'Kay,' he heard Newsome say: some invitation perhaps to intervene.

Yet he heard nothing.

He couldn't make his feelings real.

'I think I'm all right,' he said. 'I'd better go.'

'I'll drive you,' Newsome said.

'Yes, all right,' he said.

He tried to find something that would hold these parts together, peering round.

'It's like being killed,' he said to Newsome as they

went to the door. 'I don't want to go. It's such a shock. I really thought I was getting better.'

He tried not to think of Kay.

Yet, as the car was pulling away, he saw her standing at the door. 'Take me back.' And as the car accelerated he called out, 'No. No. Take me back.'

They'd reached the corner of the square.

'I can't go,' he said.

'It's all right, old man,' Newsome told him and drove on.

The square disappeared.

They passed the end of Newsome's street. A terrible coolness had come over him. It was like a sweat. He felt it springing out beneath his clothes.

At the flat he said, 'It's Fowler. In the end, that's what I can't stand.' He waited for Newsome to condemn him, to extinguish that last and vital part.

'Will you be all right, then?' Newsome said. He added, 'On your own. I'll stay longer if you like.'

'No,' he said. 'I'll be all right.' He added, 'In any case, I'll be seeing her quite soon. Later in the week, I think she said.'

Yet a moment later, like a flame exploding, a fresh anguish broke out behind his eyes.

He held to a chair, saw Newsome speak, heard nothing, saw, dissolving, the walls, the windows, the figure of Newsome finally himself, and heard, too, a vast roaring in his head, a voice, calling, as if his own, 'Kay, oh, Kay,' and felt his head consumed, eaten, taken up, as if the bone, melting, had been lifted from his brain.

'Kay, oh, Kay.'

'I should forget him: Fowler. I should forget him,' Newsome said.

And yet a moment later he heard the voice again, 'I should forget him: Fowler,' and, 'I should forget him: Fowler,' yet again, and then, 'In any case, by the end of the week, you'll be able to see her.'

'I shall see her. I shall see her. I can always talk to her,' he said, and then, 'I shall see her, I suppose,' and brought back, through a vague image of her, a faint coolness, a stillness, so that once more the walls, the windows, the curtains, the room, even Newsome, took on a recognizable shape. 'I shall see her, I suppose,' he said. 'After all, I suppose too much has passed between us. If she decides against it, I shall go away.'

'Fowler, in any case,' Newsome said, 'has left.'

'Has he?' he said.

'I'm not sure whether Kay would have wanted me to tell you.'

'Wouldn't she?' he said. 'It's not because he's gone away that I'd go and see her.' Yet he felt, as if across a chasm, the heat and the flames leap up again.

'Will you be all right, then?' Newsome said, and added, stooping down towards him, 'Will you be all right, then? Or would you prefer it if I stayed?'

'No,' he said. 'I'll be all right.'

He watched him drive off then down the street.

He lay down on the floor. He felt like a stone. He lay quite still.

He looked up, finally, towards the windows: the light, grey, ochrish, expanded slowly behind the panes.

He rang her again a few days later and asked her if she would see him.

'Yes,' she said.

183

'In the evening.'

'Yes,' she said. 'I'd like that.'

'Are you sure?'

'Yes,' she said. 'I'm certain.'

When he arrived she was sitting at the table. The curtains were still undrawn: the flowers were visible outside in the light that streamed from the window.

She sat facing the window. This had always amazed him, the lightness of the back and shoulders, the fragility beneath the dress: the thinness of her neck. It corresponded in some peculiar way to his own muscularity, that blank, uncalculating strength.

'Marjorie let me in,' he said.

'Has she gone?' she said.

'Yes,' he said.

He stood in the centre of the room, looking round. To one side, below Newsome's picture, stood his flowers in a vase.

'Are the children in bed?'

'Yes,' she said.

He sat down. He didn't take off his coat.

He could see her face reflected in the darkening window. It was small and still. The shadows hid its expression.

'I'm glad I could come back,' he said.

'Yes.'

She'd got up. 'Would you like something to drink?'

'I don't know,' he said. 'Perhaps some tea.'

She went to the stove across the room. He watched her. This, perhaps, was what he had always recognized in her: her compactness, the way she carried everything around with her, her vulnerability, her correctness, her incapacities; her general air of goodwill.

He wondered he hadn't seen it before. The thing was held inside her.

184

'I don't know what to say,' he said. 'I didn't imagine this happening.' After a while he added, 'I want to come home. That's all I have to say.'

She was gazing at the floor. This she already knew, it seemed; or at least this was an event so far off as not to concern her.

But after a moment she looked up and said, 'Yes, then. All right.'

He gazed at her quite blankly.

For a while they sat across the room.

One of the children got up: the youngest girl appeared in the door, her face white with sleep, her eyes half-closed, gazing round. She crossed to the tap, poured herself a drink, then returned to the door. 'Goodnight,' she said as she closed it.

Finally, when he judged it was time to leave, he said, 'I'll come and see you again in the evening. If that's all right.'

'Yes,' she said.

'At the end of the week.'

'Yes.'

She came with him to the door.

'Goodnight,' she said.

'Goodnight.'

When he reached the corner of the square he turned and waved and, after a moment, she waved herself and stepped inside.

PART III

Thirteen

In the summer he visited his parents.

Though he had warned them of his visit, his father was in bed when he arrived.

He sat in the living room with his mother, drinking tea, looking out through the back window at the overgrown garden and the field between the houses, its grass long now and almost hiding the fences.

He could hear his father turning on the bed, above their heads, the springs creaking, the floor groaning beneath the weight.

'He'll be down in a minute,' his mother said intermittently, as if this delay had been pre-arranged.

The whole house had a kind of weariness, like a battlefield, the windows open to the summer heat, the fire empty, the furniture pushed back to allow in the air.

His mother sat close to the table, during the long silences gazing at the floor, clearing her throat.

'Well, I'd better go up and tell him you're here,' she said eventually.

'He'll come down,' he said, 'in his own time.'

He felt his mother's presence acutely, a kind of animality, dull, uncomprehending, locked in its own kind of inconclusiveness: the slow alarm that had gradually overwhelmed her as she watched her family growing up, startled, seeing them slowly replace her in significance and purpose, and saying, 'So this is how it happens.'

In a way, she seemed the least affected of them all, as if through all the misery and desolation she had clung to the one thing she knew: the flesh and blood, my son, my son. In a way, for her, nothing had happened to him since he had been born: marriage, love, work, children; things ended very much as they began. She sat unmoved, unmoving, at the table, gazing at the floor, embarrassed perhaps by the silence, yet content they had a focus above their heads.

When his father came down he saw easily enough the signs, almost the signature, of his father's illness, a kind of self-immolation, as if he'd buried himself underground, bricked up the tunnel, refusing even now to acknowledge that he'd been released, let out.

His dark eyes looked round the room, to one side then another, and when his mother said, 'Are you looking for something?' he said, 'No, no,' and shook his head.

He'd dressed himself in a working shirt and trousers and put on a pair of socks.

'I'll make some fresh tea,' his mother said.

His father sat down in a chair by the open window, looking out at the children playing in the field.

He was very thin. The skin was sucked in about his cheeks, his eyes black and lifeless.

For a while he wondered if they would speak at all.

'How's Kay?' he said eventually, still looking towards the window.

'She's well.'

'And the kiddies?'

'They're well, too.'

'It's a wonder,' he said. Some slow shock crept into his voice.

'Yes,' he said. 'We've been lucky.'

'Lucky?' For the first time his father glanced at him. His illness flashed across his eyes, a kind of blankness.

'Luck,' he said. 'You call that luck?'

He listened for a moment to his mother rooting in the kitchen, wondering if his father might spring across at him.

'I didn't come,' he said, 'to argue.'

'No,' he said. 'I know why you came.' He looked back to the window.

'Well, then,' he said. 'That makes it easier.'

'Oh, I know,' he said. 'Easier. It does make things easier. Everything's been made easier for you. Me flat on my belly half my life has been easier for you. Kay looking after your children while you park off with some woman. I see it all, don't worry. Nothing, not even if you had begged for it, could have been easier for you. Your life's been so easy I'm surprised you're sitting there at all.'

He looked away. Then he looked at the surface of the table, polished obsessively to a glassy shine.

'Don't worry, I know why you came back here,' his father said. 'The same reason you went back to Kay. She's a fool to have you. She's sillier than I ever thought. If she only knew she's making it easier for you to go the next time.'

'Before, you wanted me to go back to Kay at any price.'

'Don't worry,' he said. 'I know.'

His mother came back in, bringing a fresh tray of cups and saucers and some pieces of cake.

'You should let Colin have his say,' she said.

'You're another one,' he said. 'I might have known.' Yet he didn't seem to attach much weight to this, for he got up and went to the fireplace and picked up his cigarettes. 'Anyway,' he said, 'as far as I'm concerned, it's finished. He

191

runs his own life. If he wants to go chasing women, and she's daft enough to let him, then that's their look out.'

'He hasn't been chasing women,' his mother said.

'Do you think I was born yesterday?' his father said. 'For God's sake. Don't you think I don't know what it's all about?'

He went back to his chair but didn't sit down.

'Anyway,' he said, 'it's got nought to do with me. I'm too old for one thing. And for another,' he flung out his arm, 'I reckon nothing to somebody who smashes up other people's lives and then comes back to say he's sorry.'

'Ah, well,' he said.

'Aye, and well it is,' his father said and lit the cigarette with his home-made lighter. A moment later he stubbed out the cigarette and said to his wife, 'Don't you think I don't know why he's gone back home?'

'I don't know,' she said.

'His conscience. He can't bear to live with it himself. He comes back here as happy as you please. "Sorry." You're as daft as he is if you believe that, for one second.'

He stood aimlessly by his chair, looking round.

'Don't worry,' he said. 'You don't have to come back here to explain.'

Pasmore glanced up at his mother. She stood, her hands clenched together, by the table, the tea and the cakes untouched beside her.

'You seem to think,' his father said, 'that you're a race apart. You're not. You're the same as me. I don't know what you've come here for.'

'No,' he said. 'I'm beginning to wonder.'

His sisters came a little later, arriving together in Wendy's car. The argument was dropped.

Some more tea was made. His father sat silently across

the room, refusing to leave, or to be involved, refusing to be disturbed at all, smoking again, his chair turned to the window where, with a kind of fury, he watched a group of children playing in the field.

'Wendy's election for the Council comes up in the autumn,' his mother said, glancing at her youngest daughter who, in a white straw hat and a summer dress, sat across the room. His mother was invariably astonished by her daughters as if, unlike her son, she saw no connection between them, their flowering, independent selves, and her own stoical, domesticated body. Perhaps this was less true of Eileen whose life, in some respects, was very much a reflection of her own and who now sat in an upright chair by the door, her hands on her knees, not unlike a man.

'Well, it comes up,' Wendy said. 'It doesn't mean I'll be elected.'

'In a ward where they have a socialist majority,' his mother said.

'Socialist,' his father said at last, to the window. 'With all that money I'd call that a paradox.'

'You're not against that too?' his mother said.

'No, I'm not against it,' he said. 'I wish her well.'

Wendy looked across at her father. She had scarcely acknowledged him, or he her, since her arrival in the room. 'Well,' she said, 'that's just the encouragement I want.'

He recognized her helplessness; in a way she'd fulfilled all his father's dreams and yet, because she was a woman, had fulfilled none of them. She was an embarrassment, a liability: without children, wealthy, apparently enlightened. It was as if her sex disgusted him.

'Oh, he's proud of you enough,' Eileen said from the door, 'when you're not here.'

'Aye. That's true,' he said, anxious not to provoke her.

193

When Jack came there was a sudden, unmistakable relief in the room.

His father scarcely looked up when his son-in-law came in, his thin face nervously alight, anxious. 'Well, this is a fair sight,' he said from the door, looking round at the family.

He nodded at Pasmore and said, 'Well, how are you, then? All right?'

'Yes,' he said. 'Much the same.'

'And how's the old man?' he said.

'Oh, all right,' his father said, looking up as if he suspected the sentiment of this enquiry.

'They haven't told you, Colin?' he said. 'Dad had a fall.'

'It wasn't anything,' his father said.

'At work,' Jack said as if, helplessly, once set on this course, he couldn't stop.

'Well,' Eileen had said. 'We'll have to be going.' To Pasmore she added, 'I have to see to the lads. It's not often I get a minute, you know, like this.'

He went out with them to the gate.

'Don't mind my father,' his sister said, grasping his hand suddenly, then embracing him. Jack nodded, standing outside the gate, looking across at Wendy's car. 'He's just trying to show you what he's been through.'

'Yes,' he said.

'Ah, well,' she said. 'As for the rest, I can't tell you how glad I am.' A car passed them in the narrow road, slowing and easing its way past Wendy's limousine. 'You'll not have time to pop up before you go back?'

'I don't think so.'

'Well, look after yourself. And Kay. Give her our love. We're always thinking of you.'

194

She walked off down the road with her arm in her husband's. At the corner, as they turned up the estate, they waved.

When he went in, Wendy too was preparing to leave. She stood in front of the empty fire adjusting her hat in the mirror above the mantelpiece.

'How's Arnold?' he said, watching her face in the mirror, the delicacy with which she arranged the hat.

'Oh, he's well,' she said.

His father had left the room.

His mother stood watching her, a little helpless. So many moments like this had passed before.

There was little else to say. They waited in silence. Then, overhead, they heard their father in his room.

'Can I give you a lift?' she said.

He shook his head; he went with her to the car.

'Are you in a bad mood?' he said. Their mother watched them from the front door of the house.

'No.' She seemed surprised that he should think she was.

'I'd like you to have stayed a bit longer,' he said.

'Oh, that house isn't for me,' she said, glancing back at her mother who stood on the step, smiling, her hands clenched together.

'How are things with you?' he said.

'Very well.' She half-smiled.

He thought, then, as he watched her sitting, small and delicate, behind the wheel of the large car, that he recognized her, sadly, for the first time.

As if aware of his mood she said, through the open window, 'He couldn't even wait, you know, to see me go.'

'Well,' he said, 'he's had a lot to contend with,' surprised himself that he should try and defend him.

'Yes,' she said, then added, 'But still, this should be some consolation.' She ran her hands round the wheel, gazing out through the windscreen at the narrow road. 'I knew you'd go back,' she said.

'Yes?'

'What else is there?' She glanced up at him.

'I don't think that was the reason though,' he said.

'Well, I wouldn't pretend to understand. I'm only a politician, boy.' She laughed.

She started the engine. It scarcely made a sound.

'Good luck with your election, then,' he said.

'Thanks.' She bowed her head, engaged the gear and glanced back. 'At least, we have that in common,' she said and signalled to the house.

His mother stood in the door waving until the car was out of sight.

He went out in the evening, walking, very much as he had done before, round the town. His father was in bed when he got back.

In the night he heard his father get up, the crack of his boots on the bare floor of the scullery, the pouring of water into a pot; the preparations to go to work.

After a while there was silence. He wondered if he had left. He heard no sound at all.

He got out of bed and went down.

From the stairs he heard a whimpering, like an animal.

When he went in the living room he saw his father dressed for work, sitting by the empty fire, crying into his hands.

'Ah, now,' he said, cut through.

His father, caught in his crying, seemed unable to release himself. He stood by him, unable to move.

'Ah, come on, now,' he said.

His father raised his head. Colin had never seen him in tears before. His face was red, his eyes shrunken.

'I'd have done anything for you,' his father said. 'You know that.'

'You have done,' he said. 'You've given me a lot.'

'Aye. I know.'

'I can't mark time with it,' he said. 'I wish you'd see that.'

'Yes,' he said.

'I haven't let you down.'

'Let me down?' he said. 'If you'd have cut me heart out you couldn't have hurt me more. I'm not learned. I know nothing. I know that. But by God, if you'd chosen to hurt me on purpose you couldn't have picked a better road.'

He put his hand on his father's shoulder. He felt the hardness through the rough shirt. It was like holding a bough.

'Look,' he said. 'I don't want to hurt you.'

His father was silent. He felt him trembling beneath him, as if he were on fire.

'I'll come with you,' he said, 'to work.'

'What?' his father said.

'I'll walk with you.'

'Oh,' he said, then added, 'If you like.'

'I'll get dressed,' he said. 'I won't be a minute.'

His mother was on the landing, standing in the lighted door of his room when he went back up.

'Is he bad?' she said.

'It's all right,' he said, not sure.

His father was waiting when he went down, with his mother, in the kitchen.

'Do you want a cup of tea before you go?' she said.

197

'I'll be late,' his father said. He began to grumble.

'Oh,' he said, 'we'll manage.'

The estate was silent. It was a little before sunrise.

As they walked up the dark roads, his father's boots echoing between the houses, the light began to spread beyond the roofs, faintly at first, illuminating banks of dark cloud.

An orange sheen appeared over the hill.

They walked mostly in silence, the sky to the west lit by the flares of the colliery and the silent banks of steam.

'Well, I go in here,' his father said when they reached the yard.

Other groups of men passed them in the road, calling out, glancing curiously at him in his suit.

'I'll be gone when you get back,' he said.

He took his father's hand. He seemed numb.

'I'll come up again.'

'Aye.'

His father glanced up quickly, at his face.

'Well, I'll see you, Dad,' he said and held his hand a moment before releasing it.

His father nodded, dazed. He seemed taken up slightly from the ground.

He watched his father go off towards the black buildings near the shaft.

As he neared them he turned round, his face lit up by the orange flares.

He nodded then turned, glancing round at the other men and disappeared.

As Pasmore walked back towards the estate the light expanded overhead. Thick clouds were laid out over the houses, drawing back to a greenish haze.

He walked round for a while, past his sister's house with its closed curtains, across the top of the estate.

Rays of light spread out across the valley. A low mist stood in the valley bottom. Across the other side, the sky was dark, the light picking out the clumps of woodland and, beyond, the low contours of the hills.

When he reached home the sun had risen above the horizon and the banks of cloud had begun to move away.

His mother cooked his breakfast. She came to see him off at the station.

They sat together in the bus.

After he'd kissed her and climbed into the train she stood alone on the platform, looking up shyly.

'Well,' he said, 'take care of yourself.'

'Ah, yes.' She nodded, smiling.

They stood watching one another until the train started.

'Look after my dad,' he said, smiling, as her figure slid away.

He leaned out and waved.

She put up her hand.

The train swung out, over the buildings, and she disappeared.

It ran swiftly across the valley, over the river.

The sky had cleared.

The sun shone down across the wheatfields, yellow, almost orange, laid out between the pits.

Somewhere, underneath, was his father, lying down.

Sometimes he asked her about Fowler, at night when he couldn't sleep, or when they were out together with the children, examining her eyes, unable to follow their search backwards, like waiting at a door for a knock to be answered: to know if there were, after all, anyone inside.

He formed a curious image of him, as of an old man or a

199

child, someone beset by their incoherency and doubt. He wondered if, after all, he didn't identify a little of himself in Fowler.

'He always thought you would come back,' she said.

'Did he?' It seemed curious that he, Fowler, uncertain about so many things, should have been confident about that.

'And you?'

'I didn't,' she said. 'I suppose that was an insurance.'

'Yes,' he said.

It astonished him, that all this should be here, his wife, his family, extracted miraculously from the past, brought into the light.

Perhaps Fowler saw himself as the agent of this unearthing and had been content, once it was over, to go away. At least, this is what he understood, for one day, unannounced, he came to the house. He opened the door to find him standing on the step and, though surprised, felt almost pleased to see him.

He was deferential and quiet, smiling, looking round, shaking Kay's hand as if, for the first time, they were being introduced, stooping down to the children. He seemed clumsy. It was warm. Intermittently he wiped his face with a handkerchief which he kept in a side pocket of his suit. With the children he appeared ill-at-ease, reassured only when they, like Kay, were distracted and left him alone: he sat upright, his head averted.

It might have been a mistake, yet when he had gone he felt grateful to Fowler.

He wondered if the other man didn't despise him.

In the winter he returned to teaching. Outwardly, despite

the events of the preceding year, little had changed. He still had a regular job, a home, a wife and children; the apparatus of his life from his books to the commercial van was virtually the same. Even the despair, it seemed, persisted.

Yet something had changed. It was hard to describe. He had been on a journey. At times it seemed scarcely credible he had survived. He still dreamed of the pit and the blackness. It existed all around him, an intensity, like a presentiment of love, or violence: he found it hard to tell.

ABOUT THE AUTHOR

The son of a mineworker, David Storey was born in Yorkshire in 1933 and studied at the Slade School of Art. His first, highly successful novel, *This Sporting Life,* was published in 1960 and awarded the U. S. Macmillan Fiction Award. *Flight into Camden,* published the same year, won both the John Llewellyn Rhys Memorial Prize and the Somerset Maugham Award. *Radcliffe,* perhaps his most ambitious novel, followed in 1963. He wrote the screenplay for the film of *This Sporting Life,* and has written and directed films for television.

In addition to his novels he is the author of five highly successful plays: *The Restoration of Arnold Middleton,* winner of an Evening Standard Award for 1967, *In Celebration, The Contractor, Home,* and *The Changing Room.*